YOUR BODY IS CHANGING

Stories by Jack Pendarvis

YOUR BODY IS CHANGING

Stories by Jack Pendarvis

Hey Jessica!
Thank you! Don't
forget me!
Wr'll be back!
XXX OOO

MACADAM CAGE

MacAdam/Cage
155 Sansome Street, Suite 550
San Francisco, CA 94104
Library of Congress Cataloging-in-Publication Data

Pendarvis, Jack, 1963-
  Your body is changing : stories / by Jack Pendarvis.
    p. cm.
  ISBN 978-1-59692-234-1 (alk. paper)
  I. Title.
PS3616.E535Y68 2007
813'.6—dc22

                                                              2006103268

Paperback edition: May 2007
ISBN 978-1-59692-191-7
Printed in the United States of America.
10 9 8 7 6 5 4 3 2 1
Book and cover design by Dorothy Carico Smith

Some of the stories in this collection were previously published elsewhere, often in
somewhat different forms or with different titles:
"Courageous Blast" in *McSweeney's Internet Tendency*; "Final Remarks" in *The
Duck & Herring Co.'s Pocket Field Guide*; "Lumber Land" in *McSweeney's Quarterly*;
"Outsiders" in *The Chattahoochee Review*; "Tollbooth Confidential" in *The Oxford
American*; "The Train Going Back" in *Mississippi Review* online; various portions of
"Your Body Is Changing" in nerve.com and the anthology *A Cast of Characters*
(MacAdam/Cage, 2006).

Excerpt from Charles Fort's *Lo!* taken from *The Complete Books of Charles Fort*
(New York: Dover, 1974). *Lo!* was originally published in 1931.
Lines from Po Chu-i's poem "Resignation" taken from Arthur Waley's *Translations
from the Chinese* (Alfred A. Knopf), originally published in 1919.

Yes, Theresa.

Behold, I shew you a mystery; We shall not all sleep, but we
shall all be changed…

—*I Corinthians 15:51*

Eastern Daily Press (NORWICH), Feb. 7, 1908—that, early in the
morning of the 5th, Mr. E. S. Cannell, of Lower Hellesdon,
saw something shining on a grass bank. According to him, it
fluttered up to him, and he found that it was the explanation of
a mystery. It was a luminous owl, he said; and, as told by him,
he carried it to his home, where it died, "still luminous."

But see the *Press* of the 8th—that Mr. Cannell's dead owl
had been taken to a taxidermist, who had been interviewed. Of
course a phosphorescence of a bird, whether from decayed
wood, or feather fungi, would be independent of life or death
of the bird. Questioned as to whether the body of the owl was
luminous or not, the taxidermist said: "I have seen nothing
luminous about it."

—*Charles Fort*

CONTENTS

Lumber Land...3

Outsiders...33

Tollbooth Confidential...47

Courageous Blast...65

The Train Going Back...71

Roger Hill...75

Your Body Is Changing...85

Final Remarks...191

LUMBER LAND

1

Dudley Durden, 50, was the only reporter for the Lumber Land *Monitor* in Lumber Land, Alabama, a pine mill town owned historically by the Cuff family. His boss was 22, a concubine named Farrah with blond dreadlocks and a Chinese tattoo. That's who his BOSS was!

The newspaper office was located in a detached, early-twentieth-century private railroad car, which sat like a gazebo on the Cuff family homestead.

Dud checked in with Farrah every Monday morning.

"Any assignments this week?"

"Nope."

"Can I pick up my paycheck?"

"It's right there in front of you."

"Turns out the eczema's spread to my eyeballs," said Dud.

"Mm," said Farrah.

"Well, not my eyeballs, don't panic. My eyelids. Can you see it?"

"Nope."

"I've been told to wash my face with Johnson's baby shampoo."

"I'm doing something important," said Farrah. Dud looked. She was tracing her hand with magic marker on a piece of yellow construction paper.

"I think the baby shampoo is helping," said Dud. "Sure you can't see it?"

The pink tip of Farrah's tongue was showing as she concentrated on finishing her hand.

"You know what I thought? I thought I was scratching my jock itch and then accidentally touching my eyes. I thought I had jock eye. I really shouldn't complain. Compared to my poor wife's skin, the skin she had when she was alive, I've got it easy. Only I don't have it easy. I keep hanging up the phone with my cheek."

Farrah held up her construction paper and squinted at it. Dud could see that the magic marker had gone through and ruined the desk, but Farrah didn't seem to notice or care. "Did you know you can make a Thanksgiving turkey using this method?" she said. "If it was Thanksgiving I'd show you how. See, that's what we would call an *interesting topic*."

Dud laughed politely. "Anyhoo, there's an off button right there on the receiver and my cheek keeps pushing on it when I talk. My cheek hangs up on people, isn't that funny? Last night I was eating potato chips and one of my teeth fell out. Not a whole tooth, just about half, I would estimate. It's one of my back ones so you can't tell. It didn't hurt or bleed or anything. Want to see it? I've got it in my shirt pocket. On the inside it looks kind of like a peanut M&M with the peanut out. Guess what it smells like."

"I'd rather not."

"Bad breath. Isn't that funny?"

Farrah crumpled up her hand and threw it away.

"I know, I know, you think I should go to the dentist. I haven't been to a dentist in thirty-five years and I'm not going to start now. I already know what he would say: 'You're some dumb Alabama hick that doesn't even know how to floss your teeth.' And then he'd charge me eight hundred dollars for the privilege. It didn't hurt or bleed or anything. These potato chips were strong enough to break anybody's tooth, they were the thick kind, cooked in a kettle full of peanut oil. They're supposed to be all natural. I think I may have bulimia. In bulimia you throw up so much that the acid rots out your tooth enamel. I don't make myself throw up, though. But what if I'm throwing up a lot but I don't remember it because my mind is blocking it out? You know how they say a bulimic can look in the mirror and perceive their body as fat even though it's really skinny? What if I'm only fat in my mind? How would I know?"

"Somebody would tell you. I'd tell you if one Monday you walked in here and you weren't a big fat guy. I'd be like, no way."

"And I wouldn't believe you. That's the nature of the disease."

"You could check your humongous shirt size."

"The bulimia might be making me see the wrong shirt size. Last night I went to sleep with my left ear clogged and this morning I woke up with my right ear clogged worse than my left ear. I think the left ear has cleared up some, but it might be that the right ear is so much worse it's just making the left ear *seem* better. And that, young lady, is why they call it the Theory of Relativity. The funny thing is, every time I burp my right ear completely clears up, but only for a second. That's followed by a tremendous sucking sound, after which the clogging returns. I suppose if I could just manage to belch twenty-four hours a day, I'd have it made in the shade!"

The intercom buzzed, a message from the Big House.

"Thank God," said Farrah.

She said Three needed to see him.

Three was his private-eye name. His real name was Lombard Cuff

III. He was the "publisher"—really the dead publisher's son, who lived in the dead publisher's mansion. He had a private detective's license that he had probably bribed somebody to get. He and Farrah lived in a fantasy world as far as Dud was concerned, where Three was a tough guy ferreting out big cases and his ladylove Farrah was a champion of freedom of the press.

Dud pocketed his paycheck and headed across the big, dewy lawn to the mansion.

Three met him in the back doorway, wearing some kind of yellow suit that rich people wore. It looked so fruity and cheap that you'd have to be rich to wear it, in Dud's humble opinion.

"There he is! Come on in."

Three led Dud to the library, where the wisdom of ages stood floor to ceiling and a sideboard glittered with bottles. Three went over to pour drinks.

"Grab yourself one of those monster leather chairs the color of boeuf a la fucking bourguignonne. You won't fucking believe it. They're so fucking soft you could cut them with a spoon. Damn, I must be hungry! You want some scotch?"

"Yes, please," said Dud. He strolled and brooded along the library's endless spines.

"Neat?"

"If that's the way it's preferable. I wouldn't know."

"I could put a bow tie on it, is that neat enough?"

Three's toothless little comment was just the sort of thing that he celebrated as wry.

Dud remembered being in the train car that day when Three kept holding up his hand to shush him because a radio commentator was talking about How Hard It Is to Put Together Bookshelves or Your Plants Seem to Die No Matter How Much You Water Them or some other rotten thing that wouldn't make a monkey laugh, much less a normal human being with an IQ over moron level. Then Three explained to Dud and Farrah why the little verbal essay had been so fucking wry—he said "fucking wry" about two hundred times—while Dud and Farrah sat there nodding. After that he made them listen to a program where men and women with soft voices tried to use various words in sentences. Three was extraordinarily drunk because earlier that day two of his bloodhounds had fallen out of an airplane and he was sad about it. He played along with the radio contestants, screaming every time he messed up, like it was the radio's fault. Then the nasally local announcer came on and said to stay tuned because he'd "be right Bach." And—*and!*—he said it with a muffled self-congratulatory gurgle: "We'll be right *mmnngghhaahhnnh* Bach." Three was so thrilled by how "fucking droll" it was that he tried to call and donate ten thousand dollars in the name of his bloodhounds. Then he took about twenty minutes to explain the difference between "fucking droll" and "fucking wry."

There was, Dud imagined, a multitude of coddled, civilized semi-drunks who found nothing more comforting than the weak puns and wretched insights of NPR.

Such was the intellect that had inherited this magnificent library.

"I guess you've read all these books," said Dud.

"Oh hell no," said Three. "I just sit in here and drink and wait for a client to appear out of the fucking ether. Sometimes I'll pull out a fucking tome and take one look at the cover and put it right back. I get depressed."

"You should always judge a book by its cover," said Dud. What a comeback! It was way over Three's head.

"That's the spirit," said Three. He raised his glass. "Now come over here and let's drink to it."

You have just openly acknowledged that I have won our battle of wits, thought Dud. He sat in the chair facing Three's and picked up his glass from the end table. The scotch made his eyes water with its terrible power and he couldn't even make the rim of the glass go all the way to his mouth from fear of gagging. So he mimicked taking a sip and put it back down.

Three moved his glass so he could get to the volume he had been using as a coaster.

"*How to Knit.* Isn't that fucking charming?"

Adorable, thought Dud. He forced a successful sip of the scotch.

Three brought a knitting basket out of hiding. He bent over a bright ball of orange yarn and went to work.

"Don't you think knitting would be a fucking great gimmick for a detective? I can just imagine myself working out the intricacies of a case in my mind, as the methodical clacking of my ivory needles lulls my faculties into a meditative fucking bliss. Look, I've just about mastered the fucking chain stitch. Do you think it's gay?"

"Not in the sense you apparently mean. No, it's nice to have a hobby," said Dud. "I wish I was a rich guy who could sit around having hobbies with all the time in the world."

"You don't do shit, Dud," said Three. "No, I'm just fucking with you. I'm sure you do some goddamn thing, I just don't know what it is." Three put down the yarn. "The thing is, I snagged a client somehow. Okay, she's a friend of the monsignor down in Bayou Cottard, you know, he was golfing buddies with the old man, and anyway... there's a thing I have to do, and Farrah doesn't want me going by myself—you know women."

"I was lucky enough to have a wife until she died."

"Right. Then you know what I'm talking about. What I'm putting on the table is, how would you like to earn the money I pay you for a change? You'd be like my goon."

"I've never envisioned myself as a goon, I'm sorry to say."

"Well, envision it, baby! It's not a term of fucking approbation. It's something detectives say. Like my right-hand man, that's all. Watching my back in case everything goes blooey. It's nothing strenuous. A stakeout. We probably won't even spot the guy."

"Well, in times of extreme quiet, such as I imagine a stakeout to be, there is a slight chance I could suffer from musical hallucinations. It's a legitimate problem, documented in *The New Yorker* magazine if you don't believe me. I don't suffer from it chronically, to my knowledge, but there have been several times when I thought I might be on the verge. My ears have been clogged lately, and apparently the condition of musical hallucinations is exacerbated by the onset of deafness, from what I read in *The New Yorker* magazine."

Just as Dud expected, Three displayed no sense of recognition about *The New Yorker* magazine. His bourgeois mind was stuck somewhere at the National Public Radio level of discourse.

The scotch was tasting better now and though Three kept talking, Dud tuned him out in favor of more pleasant ruminations:

I bet I'm the only living being in Lumber Land that's even heard of *The New Yorker* magazine. But *The New Yorker* magazine doesn't want anything to do with you if you're not a so-called New Yorker.

There's this mime and this lady sitting in a fancy New York restaurant and they're holding hands across the table and the lady is saying to the mime, "We need to talk." Now that would make a damn fine cartoon. And nobody from the so-called *New Yorker* magazine even had the common courtesy to call me back. I'd like to see a better cartoon than that one about a mime. Everybody hates mimes. I bet they laughed and laughed and then they said, Oh wait, this guy's from Alabama. No way we're cutting HIM a break. What does some JERK from

ALABAMA know about MIMES? Only us sophisticated so-called New Yorkers are sophisticated enough to understand MIMES.

I bet I'm the only resident of Lumber Land, Alabama, who knows what a mime is.

You poor country hicks. It's a guy that doesn't talk.

I ought to go to the library down in Mobile and look up every issue of *The New Yorker* magazine on microfilm and make sure they never stole my idea. I bet they gave it to one of their New York artists and said, Go on ahead and do this idea, this jerk will never know, he's from Alabama so who cares how we treat him? What's he going to do? Sue *The New Yorker* magazine?

Laugh it up, boys! Wait till I write a book and they read it and say, Hey, isn't this the guy that sent us a cartoon and we didn't even care? Man, we should have latched on to him when we had the chance!

Too late, suckers.

I'm not even going to send them my other cartoon, which is an electric chair and in front of it there's a sad-looking guy with his head shaved, and he's standing by a sign that says PLEASE WAIT TO BE SEATED. Like one of those signs in a restaurant.

Three kept knitting and talking and talking about knitting. Dud had another drink and contemplated his favorite ideas.

IDEA: Helicopter Island, the mysterious island that can only be reached by helicopter

IDEA: A serial killer who is brilliantly clever

IDEA: Winston Churchill

If a man is not liberal when he is young, etc. I believe Winston Churchill said that. If he is not a conservative when, etc. I believe I could be another Winston Churchill if I wasn't born in Alabama. Why the hell not? Nothing is impossible if you really try. Hold on to your dreams and they can come true. Miracles can happen in your daily life.

All you have to do is look around. But whoever said that wasn't from Alabama.

Nobody thought much of Winston Churchill either, till he rose to a crisis. If I had a crisis I could rise to it. I can easily picture myself on a pile of rubble yelling, "I can hear you! And soon the terrorists will hear you!"

"So, are you with me?" said Three. "Big stakeout tonight?"

"As tempting as your offer is, I fear I may prove to be more of a liability than anything. Last night my right arm became completely numb for over twenty minutes. I don't want to speculate, but I can only assume it was some sort of reverse heart attack. Now if you *really* think..."

"Look. Forget it," said Three. "I thought it would be cool."

2

Dud was sitting in his house, thinking about how embarrassing it would be to die there. He imagined some ambulance driver carefully picking his way through the squalor so as not to contract tetanus and saying something like, "Pee-yew! No wonder he died! What a dump!" and so on. Ambulance drivers and others acquainted with death on a daily basis were known to make just such sarcastic quips on supposedly solemn occasions.

The phone rang. Dud kicked around in the papers and junk on his floor, looking for it. Finally it stopped ringing.

About twenty minutes later, as darkness fell, Dud was still sitting there and a car pulled up outside. Dud's scalp vibrated. He puked up a little something but swallowed it down before it could get out of his mouth. Who was it? A maniac come to kill him? It was the only scenario he could imagine. Dud reached over and turned off the lamp.

Three knocked on his door, yelling, "Come on, Dud, I just saw you turn off the lights." Dud opened up, just a crack.

"Can I come in?" said Three. "What stinks?"

"Earlier I was cooking some exotic cuisine," said Dud. "You're probably picking up on the unusual spices."

"Are you going to let me in?"

"I'm not prepared for visitations. I'm busy working on my novel about the tragic suicides of famous people."

"Well, just put on some pants and come on out, then. I swore to Farrah I'd take you with me on this fucking stakeout, okay? Look, I'll put an extra two hundred in the kitty next week, how does that grab you?"

Dud squeezed out and shut the door quickly behind him. "These *are* my pants, by the way," he said. "The official short hiking pants of a Scoutmaster."

Three laughed. "You're no fucking Scoutmaster," he said.

"No, I happened to buy these at an estate sale, during a visit my late wife and I made to the Bluegrass State, Kentucky, shortly before her demise."

"Well, they look good on you," said Three. "Do you mind if I smoke part of a joint before we get started?" He leaned on one of the two white plaster pillars that seemed to be supporting Dud's sagging porch. The pillar fell over and rolled into the yard, and Three nearly fell with it. When he straightened himself, his downy yellow bangs were hanging in his eyes.

"Whoa!" he said.

"Don't worry, that hasn't been attached in years," said Dud. "I backed the car into it. For reasons that are too complicated to relate, it was my late wife's fault."

"Maybe I should save this for later, huh? A reward for a job well done." Three carefully wrapped his joint in a piece of tin foil and restored it to the inner pocket of his light linen jacket. "I've got all my life to smoke this joint. So let's make it happen. We're taking your car."

"Why don't we take your car? It's much nicer."

"Exactly. Somebody's bound to notice a sweet fucking ride like that, am I right? We need a piece of crap that won't attract attention."

"I hasten to state that my decrepit Escort will certainly attract attention, albeit in an obverse way," said Dud.

"I have no fucking idea what you just said."

"Anyway, a car like yours would be equipped with GPS, wouldn't it?" said Dud. "That would come in handy in a following situation."

"Hey, why don't you be the goon and I'll be the detective? Let's go, let's go." Three snapped his fingers.

"I don't have my keys," said Dud. "They're inside."

"Well, let's go inside and get them. We're on a fucking schedule, laddie."

"Why don't you wait out here and I'll go get them?"

"I need to tinkle," said Three.

"I'd prefer you to do your business outside while I run in and get the keys," said Dud.

"Oh well," said Three. He opened the door and went in ahead of Dud, tripping over some of the collectibles on the floor. "It's as dark as a fucking tomb in here," he said.

"I live artistically. Sometimes people find it unconventional."

"Where's the toilet? Or let me guess. You pee in a Maxwell House can and leave it in the corner. Is that the way the artists do it? Jesus! How many cats do you *have*?"

"None," said Dud.

"Well your house smells like a million fucking cats, so that's weird."

While Three was in the bathroom Dud rummaged around for his car keys and thought about all the things Three was sure to notice, like the squeezed-out toothpaste tube so old that the petrified gunk leaking out of the cracks was gray, and the permanent stains in the toilet, and the hissing roaches that lived behind the mirror, and the black stuff growing along the rim of the air vent, and the basket of rotting pecans in the bathtub.

3

The subject was a Frenchman, age 32. Thin and given to wheezing. Brown hair, usually oiled. Moustache. Ornithologist. In the USA on a work visa. Distinguishing physical characteristic: a strange concavity in the middle of his chest, like a hole smoothly covered by skin, for he had been born with his heart too far to the left, nearly under his arm. His telephone voice was odd; it frequently made people ask if he was crying. Subject believed that some acoustical property, caused by the unfortunate displacement of his heart, contributed in some manner to this aural illusion.

The Frenchman's American fiancée suspected him of messing around, and furthermore of merely using her for a green card.

Three had given Dud the whole rundown while they sat in the dark outside the Hank Williams Museum in Georgiana, waiting for the subject to emerge, Three behind the steering wheel because he had insisted upon driving Dud's car.

"Keep your eyes peeled for a minute," said Three. "I'm going to knit for a while." He reached around to the back floorboard and got his knitting basket, but found it impossible to maneuver in the Escort.

"I'm not a good person," said Dud.

"What?" said Three.

"I think I'm starting to turn obsessive-compulsive. Every time I pass gas I say, 'I'm not a good person.'"

"Jesus! Crack a window."

"I told you, we can't roll the windows down. You're the one that picked this car! If I roll down the window it won't roll back up. My other compulsion is I keep refining what I would say as a guest on the television program *Inside the Actor's Studio*."

"You're no fucking actor."

"Exactly. If I were an actor, it would not be a compulsion, but mere common sense."

"So what would you say?"

"On the show? When they asked me my favorite sound, I would say, 'A barber's clippers.'"

Three thought for a minute. "You mean those electric things?" he said.

"Precisely."

Three thought for another minute. "Huh, that's pretty fucking good," he said.

"These french fries taste like fish," said Dud.

"Mine tasted like french fries."

"There's blood in the straw! Look!"

Sure enough, a thin band of red was visible through the grayish transparency of Dud's plastic straw.

"What the fuck happened?"

"This milkshake is too thick. I had to suck on it so hard it made my mouth bleed."

"You could've waited for it to thaw out a little bit."

"There's your Alabama milkshake. Too thick to drink. I read in a travel magazine about a milkshake you can get in the Caribbean. Just the right temperature. Neither too thick nor too flaccid. A delight. And scented with just a touch of tropical coconut. I ought to have known nobody would know how to make a milkshake around this hellhole."

"God, Dud, you are such a pill. I thought this was going to be fun. Some people like their milkshakes thick. Some people think it indicates the use of real ice cream. Some people, I'd say most people, believe that the thicker the milkshake the higher the quality. Most people have the patience to wait for it to fucking thaw!"

"You drank your whole drink and I haven't even drunk anything yet," said Dud.

"God, do you do anything but whine? I had a Coke, okay? If you ordered a Coke you'd be done right now too. Fuck!"

"I believe cursing to be an affectation of the elite."

"What the fuck are you talking about?"

"It's one of my columns for 'Lumberin' Around!'"

"For what the fuck?"

"I knew Farrah never mentioned it to you. It's a column I want to do for the paper, 'Lumberin' Around!' Actually, I'm glad this came up. It gives me an opportunity to pitch you. As I express it in my column, let's see. I point out that in so-called sophisticated films and videos, it is always the poor who use the fuck word constantly, gangsters and thugs and hoodlums and people of various ethnical derelictions and such. Whereas in real life I grew up poor and among ruffians of all varieties, and I found them to be a reticent and indeed a prudish lot."

"What the fuck are you talking about?"

"My father never had any money, but I recall him going over to a table of young men who were engaging in some banter—harmless banter by today's standards—because his wife and his son were in earshot. That would be myself and my mother. These were clean-cut young men who probably attended a private university from the looks of them. I remarked at the time on the niceness of their sweaters...a precocious predilection! As I put it in the column. I believe the ribaldry involved a young woman bending over and giving one and all a view of her underpants. And their description of this momentous event in their lives was so abstract and oblique that to be honest it was only about a year ago that I figured out what they were talking about. One of them said something like 'rat-a-tat-tat' and pointed his fingers like the barrels of two pistols, trying to show the urgency, I believe, with which, upon the prior occasion under discussion, his eyes had gone to the suddenly visible sliver of the young lady's underpants. You can imagine how delighted his comrades became at the randy recollection of the rowdy ruffian. That's another direct quote. But those young men obeyed my father's wishes for decorum at once, and with respect. They shushed their mouths, and shushed them tight. Whereas today one can't wander out of doors without hearing the fuck word at every public location. If a Frankenstein-like doctor were able to revive him—as I postulate happening in 'Lumberin' Around!'—my late father would no doubt have another stroke within five minutes of his resurrection, very like the one that killed him in the first place. My observation is that those using the fuck word are well-to-do whites of the educated class—stockbrokers, professors of sociology, landed gentry, people with cell phones. Using it loudly, and with a casual pride. They've watched so many movies about the poor, they've adopted this street patois. This elite Hollywood idea of a street patois."

"Hey, Dud, get the fucking stick out of your ass, man."

"Ah, yes. Well, I suppose that's the reason I haven't succeeded in the publishing world. If I had a filthy mouth like a gutter and included numerous detailed descriptions of disembowelments littered with the most vulgar profanities imaginable I guess then I would be a bestselling author."

"Yeah, uh-huh, that's probably it."

"The day Miss Tina Brown took over *The New Yorker* magazine I knew in my heart that the fuck word would writhe on its pages like a plague of locusts. These editors, they take one look and say, 'Oh, this fellow is from old working-class Alabama stock. He can't possibly use the fuck word enough to meet our quota of fuck words in this modern publishing world. Let's throw his manuscript directly in the trash can and use his return postage to mail off our water bill.' And then I suppose they have a good laugh at my expense. The Alabama rube!"

"Subject sighted! Subject sighted!"

4

"Gig Young. The guy who created Plastic Man. The actress who drowned in the toilet," said Dud.

"What the fuck are you babbling about?"

"The three persons I just named all have something very specific in common. They killed themselves. But something's bothering me. I can't recall if Spade Cooley was a murder/suicide or merely a murder."

"I've never heard of a single fucking person you're talking about," said Three.

"That'll all change when my novel comes out," said Dud.

The Frenchman had left the city and driven deep into the country, with Dud and Three following. The highway was still a highway, but it had shrunk to two narrow lanes and there were no streetlights, almost no houses. Stands of trees, broken by an occasional field or orchard.

"Did I tell you about the strange mole on my neck?" said Dud.

"Probably."

"It was just on the spot that my collar rubbed against."

"Your collarbone?"

"Why, yes. Isn't that peculiar? I never in my life, until now, realized why they call it a collarbone. It just never occurred to me to consider the derivation. Certainly it is because that bone is located in such a position as one's collar would rub against. I don't know why I never thought of it before. I truly do learn something new every day."

Three grunted.

"Anyway," said Dud, "I suppose my collar just rubbed on this strange mole every day and eventually it fell off from the sheer friction. The mole did. I got it and put it in an envelope and sealed it up. I was going to bring it to the doctor for a biopsy. But don't you know, I misplaced that envelope. Can't you just imagine when someone finds it one day? They're going to get some kind of surprise. Delightful. Anyway, I don't suppose it was cancer, knock wood, because I'm not dead yet. I don't recall what I wrote on the front of the envelope. Hey, you passed him!"

The Frenchman had turned and Three had kept going down the highway.

"Of course I passed him," said Three. "We've been the only car behind him for at least thirty minutes. If he's not suspicious yet, he will be if he sees us following him down that red dirt road. We need some tactical distance."

It was a while before they found a place to turn around. When they got back to the dirt road they saw the broken gate at its entrance, the rusty, buckshot-riddled NO TRESPASSING sign. Three switched off the headlights and started down the road, which was wide enough to accommodate no more than one car.

It had rained a few days before, and huge ruts had dried everywhere. The Escort's shocks were completely shot. The men bit their tongues, clashed their teeth, hit their heads on the roof of the car, and they were blind.

"This is the real Alabama," said Dud.

"I hate to do this," Three said. He switched on the headlights. "I'm a fucking shitty detective."

Something with flashing yellow eyes ran out in front of the car and bounded into the thicket.

"That GPS sure would come in handy about now."

"How, Dud? How the fuck would it? We don't know where the fuck we're *going*."

Dud shrugged. "I'm just saying," he said.

"I'm cracking this fucking window," said Three.

"Don't you dare!" said Dud.

"I'm fucking claustrophobic, okay? It smells like shit in here. I feel like I'm breathing your *skin*. God, why do you *sweat* so much?"

"Metabolism," said Dud.

Three cracked the window and made a big show of gasping for air. "God, it stinks worse out there than it does in here," he said.

"Alabama. Should have thought of that before you rolled down the window," said Dud. "Now it'll never go back up."

"Bullshit." Three tried to roll up the window, but was unsuccessful.

Twenty minutes later they reached the end of the road, and there was literally nothing there. The crickets, locusts, and tree frogs were deafening.

"Huh," said Three. "Where the fuck did he go?"

"He vanished," said Dud.

"Yeah, that's helpful. Well, maybe there was a turnoff some-where."

They backtracked, and indeed came upon a crossroad they had missed before.

"Which way do we go?" said Dud.

"Well, first we go one way and then we go the other way," said Three.

Taking a right, they almost immediately came to another cross-road. Three put on the brakes.

"Shit," he said. "I can see I'm going to need some inspiration."

He lit his joint and began to smoke it. Once he held it out for Dud, who declined. "Suit yourself, hotshot," said Three. The car filled with moths, horseflies, gnats, junebugs. Three sat there and smoked his joint until it was nothing but a wet little dot that hardly existed.

After that they drove for a long time, over roads of dirt, roads of oyster shell, roads of gravel, turning whenever Three got a hunch, until they ended up on a road almost too narrow for the Escort, where shrubs and stickers clawed at the doors, branches came in the window and scratched Three's face, and they saw, just up ahead of them, the Frenchman's car parked next to a stream that intersected the path. Three snapped off the lights at once and stopped the car.

"Shit," he said softly.

"Do you think he saw us?"

"I don't the fuck know, Dud. I don't even know where he is."

"It's a good thing his car was there. We could have driven right into that stream."

"I have to admit I'm kind of fucking scared," said Three in a whisper. "Maybe it's the pot."

"Maybe he's sitting up there in that dark car just waiting for us with a tire iron," said Dud.

"Stop making me paranoid. Come on, let's investigate. That's what we're here for, right? There's nothing to be scared of. I have a flashlight with me that costs four hundred dollars. I bet you anything he headed downstream. That's what people do. Go with the flow." Three paused, as if stunned. "Wow. I just realized that's where that expression comes from. I am so stoned!"

"I need you to get out of the car, please. It's going to take me about forty minutes to get your window rolled up. In fact, why don't you go without me? You probably don't want to waste any time, and you have your special flashlight…"

"Leave the window down and let's go. You're my *goon*. This is your time to *shine*, brother, when fucking danger strikes."

"I just don't feel right leaving the window down."

"Do you see where we are? Who do you think's going to want in to your shitty car anyway? Count Fucking Dracula?"

"A snapping turtle, a bat, a rabid raccoon or possum, a mosquito carrying the West Nile virus…Look at all the bugs that are already in here."

"How the fuck is a fucking *turtle* going to climb in through the window? It's completely implausible. Use your fucking noodle, man."

"What about the rusted-out holes in the floorboards?" said Dud.

"Well, then, that has nothing to do with the windows, does it, little man? Let's roll."

5

They came upon the Frenchman in a clearing defined by a circle of huge, scabby old oaks. He was alone, dressed in something like a bee-keeper's outfit. He seemed startled to see them, but only momentarily. He sprinted toward them, waving his hands.

"The light! The light!"

When he reached them, he tried to force the flashlight from Three's hand. Three struggled. The Frenchman desisted.

"I am sorry," he said. "Must turn off. We use this for light?"

He brought out an iPod, its glowing screen paused on "I Think I Love You," by the Partridge Family.

"I am sorry," said the Frenchman. "You har the honers?"

Three looked at Dud, then back at the Frenchman. "Yes," he said, "we're the honers."

"I do not think you will be…'ear, you know? I think I can come, it is late, I will bother nobody? I make a study of the birds, you know? Birds?"

"I know birds," said Three.

"I am 'unting the howl, yes? Not to 'unt bang-bang. To study. Take picture. You see 'ow I am dress? The bird see me, he think…'Ah! A tree!'"

The Frenchman seemed to wait for a response from Dud and Three, who were not forthcoming.

"It is good you 'ave appear. You can be my hinformant. 'Ave you 'ear of a howl that glow? A phosphorescent howl?"

"A phosphorescent howl," said Three. "This guy's nuttier than you," he said to Dud.

The Frenchman concentrated on his pronunciation. "Owell," he said.

"Oh! Owl. They don't glow, pal. Sorry to bust your fucking bubble."

"Yes! They do not glow. But some howl do. They 'ave been sightings, you know? People look," (here the Frenchman made binoculars of his hands to illustrate) "and see the phosphorescent howl." He applauded and jumped up and down, pretending to be a person who had just sighted a phosphorescent owl. "But it is, er, undocument? Could be, for me, an himportant discovery. I am thinking it is something the howls eat, per'ap a glow*worm* or fire*fly*, or possi*bly* a kind of mush*room*. Or could be a moss that get catched in their feather? Or phosphorescent dung of rare beetle. These are my hypothezee."

"Well, I take it you're not banging somebody out here," said Three. "Not in that outfit. Where's the zipper?"

"I do not bang the howl, bang-bang! No, very careful. Very science."

"Right. Well, knock yourself out, Monsieur Valentin."

"Ow you know my name?"

"A little howl told me," said Three.

6

"God, I'm the shittiest detective in the world. My cover is totally blown. I'm going to have to call the monsignor and...What are you doing?"

"Making sure no murderous hillbillies climbed through the open window while we were gone. Looks clear. I better check your knitting basket."

"Don't touch that! I have everything organized."

They got back on the road home.

"Did that guy seem gay to you?" said Three.

"It was hard to see him," said Dud.

"Are you listening to me? Goddamnit, I've just solved the fucking case! That guy doesn't have a fiancée. He's too fucking gay. Check it out. That lady was probably a rival scientist, or an imposter *hired* by a rival scientist. I probably did the monsignor a favor. He shouldn't be mixed up with that heartless bitch. Did you see *Chinatown*?"

"Where are we? Is this the right way?"

"I don't the fuck know, Dud. Why couldn't he have driven north to Lumber Land instead of south to Bumfuck? Did you see *Chinatown*?"

"I saw it on the big screen at its inception," said Dud. "To this day I have no idea what the grand folderol was about."

"Are you fucking kidding me? It's classic. My sister! My daughter! My sister! My daughter!"

"I need to relieve myself," said Dud. "It's an emergency."

"My sister! What? We were only like in the woods for half a fucking hour, you couldn't have gone then?"

"The need just came upon me, that's the way it happens for me. Call it a weakness. I can't help it."

"Can you wait until we find the highway?"

"I cannot. Have you ever heard of Tycho Brahe?"

"Fuck no."

"Well, I don't want to talk about what happened to him. It would make me too uncomfortable at the moment."

Three pulled off so Dud could go. When Dud returned he seemed almost at peace for a while.

"Have you ever had the problem of phosphorescent urine?" he asked, finally breaking the silence.

"Can't say that I have."

"Do you think it's common?"

"I don't really think it's a fucking problem, okay? Maybe it was the moonlight shining off it. Or maybe your subconscious mind was thinking about phosphorescent owls."

"Now you're just proving your own ignorance. I didn't think a detective was supposed to assume anything."

"Oh for fuck's sake, Dudley, have it your own fucking way. Your pee glows. Congratulations."

"What I mean is, why should you assume I was talking about my urine that I urinated just now? When in fact I was talking about my urine of several nights ago in my own bathroom in my own home. I was urinating with the light off and I noticed that my urine had a faint white phosphorescence to it."

"That could come in handy. Now could you please shut the fuck up for two minutes so maybe I could figure out where the fuck we are? You were like quiet for three minutes in a row back there and I thought

I had gone to fucking Heaven."

Dud was silent for a spell and then he made a little grunt like he had thought of something private and fascinating.

"What?"

"Huh? Oh!" Dud pretended to be surprised that Three had heard his meaningful grunt. "Oh, nothing. I was just thinking about how many great novels I could have written."

"How many?"

"Fourteen."

"Wow."

"And I'm not talking about these little skinny novels everybody writes nowadays. I refuse to read any novel that's under eight hundred pages long."

"Hey, you're deep," said Three.

"Trouble is, I can't write any of my novels until everybody I know is dead. I wrote a great one about my dead wife but I had to dispose of it out of guilt feelings. I really shouldn't blame her but I do."

"On a personal note?" said Three. "It makes me uncomfortable that you blame everything on your dead wife. I think the word I'm looking for is *un-fucking-gentlemanly*."

"That's easy for you to say. You don't have a dead wife."

"Dud, we need to talk. Did you have fun tonight?"

"Fun? What's fun? I haven't had fun in so long I don't even know what fun is."

"Did you find it pleasant being a detective's goon? Is it something you could see yourself doing in the future? Think about it. It would give you plenty of material for your writing career."

"I already have too much material. It paralyzes me as a writer. I wish I didn't have so many brilliant ideas! It's my tragic flaw. All the ideas try to get out and they jam together in my brain, causing mental stagnation."

"What I'm trying to say is, if anything like this comes up again I'll be able to use you. But you can't come around the railroad car anymore. You bother Farrah."

"Well, I highly doubt that. She appears to enjoy our little conversations."

"Yeah, well, let's just say she enjoys them so much you distract her from her work. The railroad car is off limits, man."

"What about my assignments?" said Dud. "How will I get my newspaper assignments?"

"When's the last time you had an assignment, buddy? Never?"

"Yes, technically never, I guess," said Dud.

"That's right. Look, it was in the old man's will for you to be on retainer. He thought he owed you. Or maybe he felt sorry for you, I don't know. You're like a family project or something, ever since Granddad tried to send you to manage that rubber plantation, but you freaked out and they had to turn the whole fucking ocean liner around."

"Ah, my hysterical dysentery," said Dud. "It's just as bad as real dysentery in its net effect on the soul of the sufferer."

"Maybe you're my fucking illegitimate uncle or some shit, who knows?" said Three. "But there's no reason for you to keep coming down and bothering Farrah. She just cuts and pastes stuff off the internet, that's the whole newspaper, it doesn't take a team of fucking muckrakers. And trust me, you bother her. She asked me to speak to you about this."

"May I make the suggestion that you pay me all the money at once?"

"All what money?"

"However much money you think you will pay me on this *retainer* before I die."

"When are you planning on dying, Dud?"

"In about forty years, I suppose."

"Well, that's a lot of money to pay at once."

"Yes, but it would be off your mind and I could open the sophisticated restaurant I've always dreamed of. Have I ever told you about my restaurant?"

"I'm sure you have."

"Can you describe it for me, then?"

Three gritted his teeth.

"Let me refresh your memory, assuming for the moment that it is somewhere *in* your memory, which I highly doubt because I don't believe I've mentioned this to a living soul. I used to tell my late wife about it and she found the whole idea reckless. I explained to her that owning a restaurant would free me up for the leisure time I needed to contemplate my writing activities. Of course she refused to acquiesce. Maybe you could just be a backer of my restaurant, an investor. It's called Amburger. No, don't say anything, let me describe it. All I'm going to serve is variations on the common hamburger. The signature burger, the 'Amburger,' is just that—a classic, simple hamburger. The Bamburger will be designed by Emeril Lagasse, a famous chef who says 'Bam!' a lot. The Camburger will be a cheeseburger topped with Camembert cheese. The Damburger will have a piquant dash of Tobasco—'dam' being a subtle play on the idea of damnation and hellfire. The Edamburger, and yes, you might say I'm cheating on this one a bit, phonetically speaking…"

"Are there, like, twenty-six of these?"

"The Edamburger will of course be topped with Edam cheese. The Famburger is merely a plain bun served with a side of water. I don't expect anyone to order that one. It refers to famine, of course, and may be considered a symbolic nod to political consciousness or compassionate conservatism, as I like to call it. The Gamburger is made with the meat of a chicken leg, 'gam' being old-time movie slang for a leg, particularly the leg of a gorgeous woman. My Hamburger, contrary to expectation, comes with a slice of the finest Virginia ham. The I Am Burger is made to order at the customer's personal specifications, and can include any ingredient on the menu in any combination. Or I may make it the Iamburger instead, one word, a burger with exactly five ingredients, referring to the five beats in a line of iambic pentameter, although that may be asking too much of the customer, which is why I'm leaning toward the former variation. The Jamburger utilizes home-made red-pepper jelly from my deceased wife's recipe."

"Jesus Christ! Can you shut the fuck up?" Three had screamed so loudly, and with so much fervor and sincerity, that his voice seemed to shatter, and giant globes of spit hit the steering wheel and the wind-shield and lingered on his chin.

Dud was silent for about ninety seconds. Then he gasped and cried out: "Oh, my special place!"

"What now?"

Tears were rolling out of Dud's eyes. "Something stung me on my special place," he said. "It's paralyzed! Something has paralyzed my special place, do you comprehend me? Oh God, stop the car."

"You are so full of it. What's a fucking special place?"

"It's the area between my scrotum and…"

"Thanks for sharing," Three sang in a weird, girlish voice, as if it were a phrase and an affectation that Dud should recognize. Then he said, in his normal voice, "Ouch! Oh fuck! Oh shit! Snake!"

Three pulled off the road in a hurry. He and Dud jumped out, moaning and hollering. The doors of the car were flung wide, the lights were on, the Escort kept going until it hit a tree, but Dud and Three were out, stumbling and falling, Dud into the briars and Three into the road.

"I was bitten first," said Dud. "Will you please extract the venom from my special place?"

"Are you fucking…" said Three, but could not finish his thought. He flopped in the road like a hurt bird. His hand was at his neck and blood was squirting through his fingers.

Dud tried to crawl toward Three but he couldn't feel his legs. He dug his hands into the thorny brush and pulled himself toward the road, dragging his useless bottom half behind him. The hot, needling pain had traveled up his back and into his shoulders and arms but he kept pulling. A searing nausea hit him in waves, whiting out the shape of Three, which twisted and jerked in clouds of dust. As he pulled himself across the wilderness, Dud shook his head to clear it again and again. When he reached Three, Dud gathered his poor strength and raised himself up. He cradled Three's head and upper body in his lap and prepared to suck.

"Look at me, God!" Dud said aloud to the woods. "Look at me, world! I'm rising to the crisis! I'm rising to the crisis! I'm rising to the crisis! I'm rising to the crisis!" Then he looked down at Three, whose mouth and throat had apparently frozen up in a horrible way. Something white was coming out. He was making a sound that sounded something like *Fuck*. He seemed to die.

"Great," said Dud to Three. "Thanks for nothing."

Dud lay Three's dead body on the ground. He got down beside Three and positioned his mouth on the gory throat, as if he had been selflessly sucking the poison despite his own grave wounds that were killing him as well.

I wish I could see what this looks like, he thought.

There came a sound like rushing wind and suddenly he was floating over the scene, which turned out to be just the way he had pictured it.

"Yes," said Dud. "Perfect."

OUTSIDERS

Mr. Morton Fielding, 72, wrote a humorous column entitled "Fairfielding" for the Fairfield, Connecticut, *Pennypincher*. One afternoon, the day of the first snowfall, he had taken the train into New York to meet with his estranged daughter in the dark, drowsy bar of the Essex House, a cozy hotel across from Central Park.

Before heading to the bar he had double-checked with the desk clerk to ensure that the room he had reserved for his daughter encompassed a view of the park. It made him happy to think of her, with all her troubles, being able to look out of her window at the beautiful snow on the trees.

His daughter, however, was forty-five minutes late for their appointment and Mr. Fielding fretted that she would never arrive. He sipped club soda with a wedge of lime squeezed in, picked through the complimentary nut bowl for cashews, and observed the interesting people who came and went.

At one point a large, dark, acne-scarred man—dressed in what Mr. Fielding recognized from his own experience as a United States Navy peacoat of a certain vintage, buttoned severely, all the way up— approached the small pale fellow who was seated at the table next to Mr. Fielding's. The little man stood.

"Long time," he said.

The two men shook hands and sat down. Mr. Fielding couldn't

help overhearing their conversation.

"I'm having grappa," said the little man. "You should have some."

"Okay," said the larger one.

"Take off your coat."

"I'd rather leave it on. Look at the buttons. Little eagles. I got it for a dollar at a thrift shop. Amazing. That was ten years ago. I've thrown up on this coat a lot."

"You're going to get hot."

"I'll live," said the big one.

"I know an Italian. He told me that grappa should be served freezing cold. I've never found a bar that does it that way, though."

"Oh well."

"Grappa was popular for a few years and now I don't think it's popular anymore," the smaller one said. "It's not for every taste. You should definitely try some. How have you been?"

"Doing pretty well."

"Hey, do you know that guy in the nasal-spray commercials? Do you know who I'm talking about?"

"No."

"He's in those nasal-spray commercials. He was in here just two minutes ago, I'm not kidding. See that young girl? Right there, by herself. He was trying to pick her up. It was sick. I could hear everything he was saying. He was quoting poetry. I was like, 'Hey, it's the guy in the nasal-spray commercials and he's trying to pick up a hot girl. Sick.'"

"Huh."

"Only in New York!"

There followed a long, reflective pause.

"I mean, look at us," the little man continued. "Here we are. Who would have thought it? Two Alabama boys in New York for business.

Remember all those girls who wouldn't screw us?"

"Actually I'm in New York for an art show, like I said in my email."

"Well, art is your business," said the little one.

"And what is it you're doing these days?" the larger man asked.

"Short version, I find ways for my company to make a profit off of fish species that are traditionally considered undesirable, inedible. Trash fish. Sounds dull, I know. It's what we call a 'blue ocean' opportunity. That has nothing to do with the real ocean, it's just a business phrase. It means we're carving out a section of the industry where there was no industry before, creating a whole new demand for something nobody wanted in the first place. Hey, maybe it's not art but it takes some imagination. A good deal of creative intelligence, actually."

"Right, right."

"I've heard people say it's an art in its own way. I don't pretend to be an artist of course."

"Which one's our waiter?"

"You look good. You got fat. No, that's a good thing."

"Yeah, it's great. Maybe I'll die from it."

"You're tall, so it's not as noticeable. I wouldn't worry about it." The little one snagged the waiter and ordered grappas for himself and his friend. "I invited some other people to join us," he said. "George and Mandy. You don't know them. I thought we could talk about Alabama. They're ex-pats, too. When did you get out?"

"I didn't."

"You still in Alabama? What a hoot. Why?"

"I don't know. I like to take pictures of it."

"Whoa! You're supposed to sip it, bro. It's artisanal. I'm getting a bottle for the table. Now remember to sip it, okay?"

The waiter brought over a bottle and pretty soon the little man's friends showed up. He said to them, "Ray is a full-blooded Creek Indian."

"Wow," said the woman, Mandy.

"Yeah," said Ray, the large Indian in the Navy peacoat. "Wow."

"Hey, why are you wearing that big fat coat? Aren't you hot?" Mandy asked.

"No."

"At least unbutton it," said Mandy. "Are you underdressed? I bet you feel underdressed so you don't want to take off your coat. Oh, I will call you on your shit! It's what I do. I notice things and then I call people on their shit. I can't help it."

"It's true," said George, the husband. "She will call you on your shit. This girl will call you on your shit."

"I guess it's not politically correct," said Mandy. "So be it. Oh well."

"That's why I love you, baby," said George.

"Don't you 'baby' me!"

"Ouch! You called me on my shit."

"Hey, tell 'em why you got kicked out of college," the little man said to the Indian. "Ray got kicked out of college. It's a great story."

"Are you from around Atmore?" asked George. "I bet you are."

"No."

"The Creeks have that great buffet. Have you been? I'm sure you've been. Soul food, really. Is there a Native American equivalent? Anyway, it seems like soul food to me. At the Best Western? I'm sure you've been. I think Mennonites or somebody used to run it but now it's the Creeks. The food seems the same."

"Hey, I thought Ray was going to tell us why he got kicked out of college," said Mandy.

"Oh, I fought a lot," said Ray.

"How much is a lot?"

"I did some fighting."

"What kind of fighting?"

"You know." Ray made some punching motions with his fists. "Fighting."

"Tell 'em what you did to Carl," said his little friend.

"This guy Carl kept calling me a wimp, and…Do you mind if I use some bad language?"

"Go right ahead," said Mandy. "With my blessing! What are you afraid of? Am I a frail blushing flower? I live in New York City!"

"Well, what he really kept saying was 'You *pussy*, you *pussy*,' just like that, and poking me in the chest."

"That got you aggravated."

The little fellow broke in: "You're not telling it right. They have this thing. It's called 'Two Miles of Naked Freshmen'? It's where they make all the freshmen run two miles naked and everybody stands along the road hooting at their asses."

"That doesn't sound politically correct," said Mandy. "I guess that makes me all for it! That's just the way I am. I hear that something is politically incorrect and I'm like, 'I'm there!'"

"It's a tradition," said the little guy. "Not officially sanctioned but everybody knows about it. They turn a blind eye. It's a lot of fun."

"Well, I didn't want to do it. And this guy Carl was trying to talk me into it by going, 'You *pussy*, you *pussy*,' and poking me in the chest. And he's naked. And all the freshmen are running by naked. Carl steps out of the line just to poke me in the chest and harass me. So after a few minutes I head-butted him. I mean I *head-butted* him. I cracked his head wide open. Split his forehead like a melon. And Carl started crying. He's a skinny little white punk with a nose stud and skin like a sick fish. He ran away naked, crying, with blood pouring down his face. And by now everybody else was gone, the trail was empty, and here's Carl running naked *by himself* down the empty trail, crying and with a bleeding head, with his hands out in front of him kind of limp like this."

"That's quite a picture you put in my head," said Mandy. "My goodness. I do declare."

"Another time a guy tried to steal my backpack and I jumped up and down on his crotch."

"Where *are* you from then?" said George, pouncing on Ray's last syllable. He was the queasy type, Mr. Fielding observed. Mr. Fielding was hoping they would say something a little less off-color, something he could use in his humor column. And when his daughter arrived he could casually mention it to break the ice.

"You're not from Atmore, so where are you from?" said George.

"Oh. Bayou Cottard," said Ray.

"Oh my God. You must be the only good thing that ever came out of Bayou Cottard," said Mandy.

"Are you from there too?" said Ray.

"Oh God no. No way. Bayou Cottard Day. Remember that?"

"It's a joke we have in our family," George said. "My father nearly sawed off his hand building a deck, so he had to go to the emergency room. And he said that it seemed like nearly everybody there was some redneck from Bayou Cottard who had had some kind of stupid redneck accident. He called it Bayou Cottard Day. We still say it all the time because it's so hilarious. You know, when I'm down there for Christmas or whatever and we're at the Target and there are a lot of rednecks around."

"Bayou Cottard Day!" said Mandy.

"Who needs more grappa?" said the little grappa fiend. He filled the empty glasses.

"Well, anyway, you got the hell out," said George. "That's good. 'Good on you!' like they say in Australia. 'Good on you, mate!' Tim says you snap photos, right? I think that's great. What of?"

"Poor people," said Ray.

"That must be hilarious! We have to check it out. Hey, I know what you would like. You ever see that one part on Jay Leno? He gets these funny-looking goobers to show how dumb they are right there on national TV. Like he'll ask some bucktoothed freak with his hair sticking up what's the capital of something and they won't even know what he's talking about. Or he'll show them a picture of a famous king and they'll say, 'Who's that?' It's hilarious."

"Isn't that funny, I don't even know what Jay Leno looks like," said Mandy. "That's just how little television I watch. Someone mentioned to me—it was probably you, George, don't deny it!—that Jay Leno was retiring and I had to admit I couldn't even picture the man, much less recall his particular accomplishment. Isn't that just dreadful of me? People become intimidated when they realize that my opinions are so uninformed when it comes to television. I'm sorry, but I'm not sure I'll even understand your photography. I'm afraid I won't know the pop-culture references that you're skewering."

"I'm not skewering anything," said Ray.

"Well, I'm afraid I just won't get it. I don't even know who Jay Leno is!"

"It has nothing to do with Jay Leno."

"Is that his name? Is that how it's pronounced? Who *is* he? Seriously, somebody tell me. No, no, I changed my mind, I don't want to know. I'll remain ignorant, thank you very much! If that's what passes for ignorance in this misbegotten nation then sign me up."

"It's like me drinking grappa," said the little one. "You ought to see the looks I get from waiters! Grappa is no longer trendy. So what? I happen to like grappa. These waiters can't believe their eyes. Who does this guy think he is, ordering grappa? It should be served freezing cold. My Italian told me. But they won't do it. We should get another bottle."

"Yes, it's exactly like that!" said Mandy. "People can't believe it when I say I refuse to sell my art in a gallery. I'm just not interested in that world. Really I don't understand that impulse at all. I mean, why would you want to put what you do on *display*?"

"So people can look at it," said Ray.

"You see, that just doesn't interest me at all. People can't believe it when I say that. You probably think I'm a horrible person, putting down your way of life right to your face. I won't apologize, though, no matter how hard you beg me."

"It's true, she won't," said George. "All she can do is call you on your shit. It's in her nature."

"What's your medium?" Ray asked Mandy.

"I don't have a medium."

"I mean, do you paint, or...?"

"I know what you *mean*," said Mandy. "I know what a *medium* is. I'm not some *redneck*. If you'd let me explain...Art can be the way I sit, the way I talk, the way I comb my hair...The only reason I would do art is to destroy it from the inside. Otherwise I couldn't be bothered with the hassle. Paying an agent ten percent, for what? Dealing with people trying to change who I am. I refuse. I simply refuse. Am I blowing your mind? I also don't like people named Joan or Joanne or any song with the word 'ghost' in it. I'm sorry if that freaks you out, but I just have to be honest. That's what people can't handle."

The waiter brought over another bottle of grappa and some fresh glasses.

"So, Ray, what's your fascination with the po' folks? Is it that Bayou Cottard connection?" said George. "I would think you'd want to *avoid* them, if anything. Hey, does anybody want to pay money for a picture of poor people? Where're they going to hang it? Over their dining room table so they can contemplate on it while they eat?"

"I would feel so depressed," said Mandy.

"It's not only poor people," said Ray. "Maybe that was a bad description."

"My father was an emergency room doctor," said Mandy. "Not the same emergency room that George's father went to, of course. This was back in Louisiana when I was ten years old. But it's the same white-trash factor. My father was a brilliant emergency room doctor and he got so tired of helping these rednecks. Do you know that not one redneck whose head he stitched up ever thanked him? Not one."

"Tell him about the gas pump," said George.

"What about a gas pump?" said Ray.

"You know what my father saw this one redneck doing at a gas pump?"

"Smoking a cigarette?" said Ray.

"How did you know?"

"I don't know, I just guessed. Something about the way you said it."

"Well, that's right. There was this redneck smoking a cigarette at a gas pump and my father went ballistic on his ass. 'Listen here, you stupid redneck...' You know. That redneck couldn't believe that somebody was calling him on his shit. He just stood there with his cigarette hanging out of his stupid mouth."

The Indian murmured.

"Did you say something?" asked his friend.

"Huh?"

"I thought you said something."

"Yes, let's hear from the artist," said Mandy.

"By all means," said George.

"I was a bully all the way from fourth grade to about tenth grade," said Ray. "Eleventh and twelfth too, but I was starting to get a handle on it. Every time I beat somebody up I'd cry about it later. Looking back, I feel worse about the mental abuse I laid on people than the beatings I handed out. I have to say, though, it's a great feeling when you get to that point of no return. When you get to that point of, 'I am going to hurt you now, and hurt you bad, and that's all there is to it and there's nothing anybody can do about it.'"

"How violent," said Mandy.

"I remember being at Gulf Shores when I was twelve, when my stepbrother tried to turn the truck around and got it stuck in a stranger's yard. Yard was nothing but beach sand. You can really get stuck.

"I looked up to my stepbrother. He was a lot older than me. Man, he was tough. Navy Seal. He tried to explain how to help get the truck unstuck but I couldn't do anything right and he was getting pissed. Then two Yankees with red faces and white hair and these weird bluish legs came out of the house and asked what the trouble was.

"One of them told us it was just like pulling a truck out of the snow, hadn't we ever pulled a truck out of the snow? My stepbrother said he had never pulled a truck out of the snow.

"Well, that really set them off. These Yankees seemed to get some good fun out of the fact that we had never pulled a truck out of the snow. They couldn't believe there was a grown man who had never pulled a truck out of the snow."

"I always think it's hilarious when Southerners complain about an inch of snow," said the Indian's small friend. "They should try living in New York for a day!"

"Now it's funny you should say that," Ray said. "That's just the tack these Yankees took. One of the Yankees had been in Mobile during a little snowfall. He told us how the city of Mobile had shut down completely in a state of panic, and the snow wasn't even sticking to the ground."

"That's just how it was down there!" said the little one, laughing.

"Yes," said Ray, "the Yankee had it all down pat, all right. The way people raided grocery stores for supplies, how the City of Mobile got the snowplows out...Then he described his own more rational reaction to the snow, which had been to conspicuously ignore it."

"That's hilarious!" said George. "I bet those rednecks were like, 'Do what?' Like, 'What's this white shit, Bubba?'"

"Bayou Cottard Day!" said Mandy.

"The main Yankee, as I recall, expressed alarm at the way Mobilians began donning overcoats and woolen caps whenever the weather hit forty degrees. He said that he prided himself on marching up and down the sidewalk in shorts and sandals at such a time, and then when someone asked him wasn't he cold he would say, 'This is nothing!' and everyone would be thrilled and amazed at his high level of comfort. Then he described some snow that had come up past the windows of his house in Wisconsin and had also smothered a cow."

"Now that's snow," said George. "What you get in Alabama is not snow. I don't know what it is, but it's not snow."

"Bayou Cottard Day!"

"One of the Yankees got a large rope and told me to tie it under the truck. I crawled under the truck. I didn't know where to tie the damn rope. I didn't know how to make a decent knot, even. One of the Yankees scooted in to the rescue and started showing me how to tie it. He was smiling like I was a retarded child, you know, very nicely.

"Finally they got the truck out—my stepbrother and I ended up not doing anything, they really did all of the work—and they stood in the sand waving goodbye and my stepbrother told me to roll down my window. He leaned across me and yelled at 'em like, 'I'd like to see you in an asphalt parking lot in Mobile when it's a hundred degrees and a hundred percent humidity! I'd be saying what's the matter? Why are you laying on the ground with a stroke? Ain't you ever been in a hundred percent humidity before? Wouldn't that be funny?'

"One of the Yankees said, 'You're welcome,' you know, real dry. My stepbrother got out of the truck and tried to beat their heads in with a tripod. Did I mention he was a photographer? Yeah, he was my inspiration in that matter. He never got to do anything with it because he went to prison. I've always felt like I was kind of taking up the slack for him. He sacrificed a lot for me. Hell, this is his peacoat. That's why I never take it off. I feel like I been spending my whole life trying to grow into it."

"You said you got it at a yard sale," said the little man.

"I said a thrift store. I lied. I don't like talking about my stepbrother."

"Is he still in prison?" said Mandy.

"He died in prison," said Ray. "Stabbed through the heart."

"Oh my God. What was he there for?"

"Killing those Yankees," said Ray. "He only killed one. But he pleaded guilty to both."

"Why?" said Mandy.

"Because I killed the other one," said Ray.

Mandy made a small burping sound, like some grappa had come up from her stomach and she had swallowed it again.

"I was trying to help him. He chased them up these tall rickety steps into their beach house, you know, the house was up on stilts because of hurricanes and high tides and floods. By the time I got the nerve to climb on up and peep inside, one of the Yankees was laying on the floor and my stepbrother had the other one flung over the arm of a couch, garroting him with fishing line. I found out later it was fishing line. He really should have used the rope from the truck."

"Oh my Jesus Christ," said George.

"But that rope was kind of thick. My stepbrother was a Navy Seal, you know. The white United States government taught him all these techniques. He was trained to kill without thinking twice about it. He's finishing off the one Yankee and the other Yankee starts coming to. On the floor with this brown blood all around his head, that's what I thought at the time, that it looked brown, I thought, 'White people have brown blood, huh.' And there was, there was a yellow rag, a plain yellow washrag on an end table, next to a spray can of Lemon Pledge, and I don't know, I grabbed that rag and shoved it in the Yankee's mouth to keep him from making noise. And I pinched his nose shut like this."

Ray made a feeble grab at his friend's nose. His friend jerked back in his chair.

"I should have eaten something today," said Mandy. "I…" She stood swiftly, knocking over her chair, and fell forward. She braced herself with her palms against the table.

"No, wait, don't go," said Ray. "I have something I want to show you. Something I'm never without."

He reached into the pocket of the peacoat and tossed onto the table something that looked from Mr. Fielding's point of view like a piece of modern art: a stiffened yellow rag for a canvas, clotted and crusted with red-brown stains and splashes.

Mandy clapped her hand over her mouth.

"No, I'm just shitting you," said Ray. "I had a nosebleed this morning." He laughed. "What's the matter, aren't you going to call me on my shit? I don't even have a stepbrother."

As Mandy tried to leave the table she tumbled to the floor and lay there with the back of her legs showing and her lovely hair in disarray.

Mr. Fielding rose.

"You deliberately tripped that young woman," he said to Ray. "By

God you did. I make myself available as a witness."

Ray stood up. "Sir, I did no such thing," he said.

Mr. Fielding grew livid and wild. He made noises like a snake.

Ray approached him.

George scrabbled for the exit, leaving his wife cringing and slobbering on the floor. The little man studied his grappa bottle, held it up
to see if a swallow was left, and seemed in all to be pretending that he
was uninvolved with the incident, and indeed with the world. The bartender was on the phone to 911. Waiters posed about the bar like expec-
tant ninjas. Ray had gotten Mr. Fielding from behind and seemed to be
shaking him like a bottle of Coke until a nut flew out of Mr. Fielding's
mouth.

The EMTs, when they arrived, discovered that Ray, in his gusto to
save Mr. Fielding from choking, had broken three of the old man's
brittle ribs. There was some talk, eventually dismissed, that Ray might
have demonstrated glee, during the rescue, in applying just a little more
force than necessary. One of the ribs had punctured Mr. Fielding's right
lung, happily not resulting in death.

During his first few days in the hospital Mr. Fielding remained particularly addled and insisted again and again that the nurses check on
his daughter. He seemed to believe that he had been injured in her
defense, when in fact she never arrived.

TOLLBOOTH CONFIDENTIAL

Here is a conversation I had with a big, strong black woman. She wanted to hire somebody and I needed to be hired. The first thing she asked me was why they let me go from the Earthly Garden of Tea.

"That was a misunderstanding," I said. "A woman complained that her tea cookies were broken and I said, 'Lady, they taste the same broken as they do whole.' She was one of the corporate owners from Florida, on an undercover inspection. She didn't like my attitude. She also saw me smart off to an old man, she said."

"Did you?"

"Smart off? An old man was trying to tell me how to make change the old-fashioned way. I didn't care. I told him we have computers for that now. I explained very patiently that he got the same amount of change whether I counted it out the old-fashioned way or whether a computer counted it for me, so why did he want to get in my face about it? He should be happy to be in a place where the price is reasonable and you get some change back from your hard-earned money. That was considered smarting off, apparently."

"You realize, don't you, that your job here would involve making change?"

"Well, yeah, but it's fifty cents to go through the tollbooth, right? Like if somebody hands me fifty dollars, I give them back forty-nine fifty. I could do that all day."

"Let me be clear. The position that's open is a cashier position. There's a lot more customer contact than if you were occupying, say, an exact change booth, where the driver merely tosses his coins into the sorter basket and the arm rises automatically. You will have to accept the customer's cash with complete courtesy and give him his change quickly and efficiently. Any slowness or discourtesy on your part could result in a traffic accident or even death. That's the difference between working at a tollbooth and working at a place that sells cookies."

"And jellybeans. I could always guess somebody's favorite jelly-bean flavor without them even telling me. It made me popular with the customers. I was giving them something extra. I was appreciated, until the unfortunate incident."

"Moving on, you didn't remain employed at the Video King for very long."

"I was literally robbed by gypsies. One of them distracted me with a question about the California Raisins after I already had the cash drawer open. Anyway, I wasn't fired. The investigating officer gave me a hard time, like I was lying, and the assistant manager didn't say so, but I could tell she was taking his side. So I turned in my notice with a sense of indignation. It was the right thing to do and I stand by it."

"When's the last time you shaved, son?"

"I shaved for my twenty-fifth birthday."

"And how old are you now?"

"Thirty."

"Your beard makes you look a lot older than thirty."

"Thank you, ma'am."

"Uh-huh...Honestly I'm surprised it's been growing for...five years, is it?"

"It'll be six years in May. I'm going on thirty-one. I'm a Taurus."

"Seems like it would be down to your knees by now."

"Oh, no ma'am. My beard grows outward, slowly outward, rather than downward. And as you can see, it curls inward on itself not unlike pubic hair, if you'll pardon the expression."

"Actually it's just the expression that came to my mind. Our tollbooth attendants are required to be clean-shaven. Is that a problem for you?"

"Well...yes...that's a problem. I used to be in a Dixieland band and we all have beards. There's a chance we might get back together if I can iron some things out."

"You're a skinny white boy. How skinny are you?"

"I'm one hundred twenty pounds and five feet ten inches tall, ma'am."

"You know, I believe I have a uniform that will fit you, just about."

"I can't shave my beard. Some of the other guys have, but I think that shows a sense of pessimism, and I don't want to fall prey to that."

"I have a special job for you, son. You won't have to shave your beard. I have a feeling about you. I had a feeling when I read your résumé and now that I've met you I know my feeling was right. This is not the cashier position I'm talking about now. This is a job that will last you just until four o'clock or so today, and it pays two hundred dollars. Are you interested?"

"Two hundred dollars for one day?"

"For less than one day."

Sometime between 10:00 a.m. and 4:30 p.m., a man was going to pull up to a certain tollbooth in a Volvo station wagon. He was going to say, "All I have is a Sacajawea dollar," and I was supposed to give him a package and let him through.

The woman shut the blinds and made me put on, over my clothes, the bulky tan jumpsuit of a city maintenance worker. It was a disguise. When I walked out, nobody looked at me twice. With the package concealed in my otherwise empty toolbox, I walked out of the building and about fifty yards to my post on the highway: the sixth booth, an exact change booth, the one with the broken camera that I was supposedly there to fix.

There was a window of fog-colored acrylic on either side of the tollbooth, which meant that I had two lanes to keep my eye on. Each window was equipped with a little speaker, like at a bank, and a drawer like the one Hannibal Lecter used in *Silence of the Lambs* when he wanted to pass notes and stuff to Jodie Foster. The tollbooth seemed to be about the size of a coffin. In any case it had very few attractive features and did not seem like a fun place to work. It was damaged. Some of its insides seemed to have been removed. There was nowhere to sit. A red phone hung on the wall, and a shelf where you could put things. There was a wastebasket, and a cash box, and a cheap-looking plastic megaphone, and that was about it for the features of the tollbooth, except for a keypad with numbers on it.

If someone complained that the arm was jammed, I was supposed to punch in the code "1924" and it would lift up. "1924" was easy to remember because it seemed like a date when something famous might have happened, or the year an old person might have been born.

I couldn't imagine an easier way to make two hundred dollars.

The catch was, what was in the package? Obviously it was something illegal, and possibly dangerous, or the supervisor would have handed it off herself, or she would have made one of her normal workers do it.

It was none of my business, because I had accepted the proposition and my handshake is as good as a contract. But what if the package was an explosive device designed to shut down interstate traffic, for example? I did not want any part of terrorism. That is where I draw the line.

I thought I should call Puddin', a former professional mathematician turned park ranger. Puddin's gig in Carlsbad Caverns only takes up three months of every year. The rest of the time she walks around in her apartment wearing nothing but a slip.

Puddin' has a lot of interesting characteristics. She's very small and slim and pointy all over. She is a native Hawaiian, I believe, who enjoys dyeing her hair strange colors. I like going over there and seeing her answer the door in her slip, smoking one of her cigarettes, the ones she rolls herself, a habit she acquired out west in Carlsbad Caverns. One time she was wearing a dingy white slip and a dark red pageboy haircut and she had a Band-Aid under each knee and she was standing in the doorway with her hip cocked and smoking one of her cowboy cigarettes and it was the most heartbreaking thing I have ever seen.

I wanted her advice about the package because according to Puddin', the park ranger business throws her into contact with all sorts of people on the fringe of society—hippies, punk rockers, bums, and bad apples.

There is one more thing about Puddin'. I am not sure it is germane, or even polite to bring up, but I'm going to mention it because it's so interesting. She claims to be having, or to have had already, an affair with the elderly R&B sensation Prince. The timeline is not clear.

None of us believes she knows Prince. It is obviously a huge lie. The question is, really, whether Puddin' believes it or not.

This one guy, Ed, picks on her about it. We'll all be at a nice party and Ed will say, "Hey, Puddin'. Remember when Prince changed his name to that symbol? What did he make you call him then?" And we'll all stare at him until he shuts up.

Because I mean, bottom line, Puddin' is the greatest girl ever and who cares if she likes to say she does it, or used to do it, with Prince? We all have our problems, that's my theory. The best thing to do is pretend we don't hear our friends too well when they start going on about their crazy stuff.

I picked up the red phone to call Puddin', but there weren't any buttons on it. The woman came on the line and asked what I thought I was doing.

"I have diabetic disease," I said. "I was trying to call my buddy Puddin' to bring me my medicine."

"This had best not be a trick," said the woman.

"I could faint out here and that would ruin everything," I said.

"You're in this up to your neck," she said.

"I'm not trying to squirm out of anything," I said.

"I'll call your friend for you," said the woman. "What's the number?"

I couldn't think of what to do, so I gave her the number.

"If this is a trick you'll live to regret it," she said.

Right after that a guy parked beside my booth and started yelling at me. I pushed the speaker button.

"What time is it?" I said. "I know it's not ten yet."

"What the hell are you talking about? The thing won't do right."

"Are you supposed to be in a Volvo station wagon?" I asked. "Because you're in an Infiniti."

"What are you, a freak?" he said. "I put in my money and the thing won't do right. Open it up and let me through, you freak."

"Are you sure you put in fifty cents?" I said.

"Are you sure you don't want me to push your nose in for you?" he said. "What are you going to do, arrest me over fifty cents? I make four hundred thousand dollars a year. You look like a freak." I noticed that he had an innocent child in the backseat, a child who seemed blissfully unaware of his father's hateful ways. I pushed "1924" and let the man through.

The confrontation exhausted me. I don't enjoy getting into it with people. I sat on the floor and took a nap. Cars came up in a regular stream. I listened to them idle, and then the clatter of coins in the basket, and the clunk and whir of the arm going up and down and letting the cars through. Everyone was cooperating, everything was working correctly, it made a nice picture of the world, and the steady sounds cleared my mind of conflict and allowed me to doze.

I don't know how long I rested that way before a banging disturbed me. I jumped up and grabbed the package and saw the face of Puddin' smashed comically against the window. I hustled her inside.

Puddin' was wearing a wifebeater T-shirt of white corrugated cotton, a plaid skirt that seemed to be held together by a safety pin, and fishnet hose. Her hair was dyed bright white and she had on gray lipstick. Puddin' is young, and goes through a lot of phases.

"Crouch down," I said. "Where'd you come from?"

"India brought me in her van," said Puddin'.

"Did anybody see you?"

"Yeah, lots of people. I looked in almost every other tollbooth before I found you. I almost got run over twice. Are you sick?"

"No."

"I had a weird message on my voice mail. Somebody said you were sick. Do you need some Xanax?"

Even though she was in an awkward position she managed to wiggle out of her fluorescent pink backpack and kindly tried to dig out some Xanax for me.

"It was nice of you to come," I said. "You're a real trooper, Puddin'."

"What are we doing out here?" said Puddin'.

"Just stay low to the floor like that and don't let anybody see you."

I handed down the package, which was about the size and shape of a big book, wrapped tightly in newspaper.

"I want you to tell me what this is," I said. "I want to know what kind of funny business I'm mixed up in."

"You need to clip your nails," she said.

"Mom usually trims them, but she's been busy this week," I explained. "Moms have lives, too, you know."

Puddin' acted surprised that Mom trims my nails. She didn't say it. Her face said it all.

"I thought we could tell each other anything," I said.

"Not that," said Puddin'.

Her back was against the tollbooth wall and her knees were up in the air, making her skirt fall in such a way that I noticed how her fishnet hose were being held up by garters. I forgot about the package for a minute and we did some things on the floor of the tollbooth that it might not be fitting to mention.

We weren't really on the floor because there was no room to stretch out. I guess I can say we were in kind of a sitting position although I don't want to get into any further detail.

I do suppose it would be okay to tell a joke on myself. At one point I was making what I assumed to be some erotic noises, which looking back were probably pitched higher than I intended. These noises, in any case, seemed to be effective, so I made them louder and more frequently until Puddin' said, "Hey."

"What?" I said.

"Can you please stop making those noises?" she said.

Suddenly I got out of the mood for whatever it was we were doing. We sat on opposite sides of the tollbooth, on the floor. I was sitting cross-legged and Puddin' had her legs out in front of her like a doll, and even though she's not very tall her feet were touching my knees. I asked her to open the package and look at it.

"Be careful, it might be a bomb," I said.

"It can't be a bomb," she said. "That isn't something God would do to me."

She opened the package and we looked at what was lying on the newspaper.

At first glance I thought it might be a block of frozen spinach. But really it was darker, like dirt, and there was an oiliness or moistness to it.

"What you have there is a brick of hash," said Puddin'.

"Is that what it is?" I said.

"Remember when Prince took me on a cruise down the Nile?" she said. "I burned a lot of hash on that trip."

"Is that the terminology?" I said.

"Let's burn some," she said.

"We can't. It doesn't belong to me."

"Who does it belong to?"

"My supervisor. Wrap it back up."

"What's your supervisor doing with a brick of hash?"

"That's not for me to say. She entrusted it to me for delivery and I gave her my word."

"You're ethical for a hash mule. Let me roll us a couple, come on. I'll pinch it right back into acceptable brick form, I swear. I'll wrap it good and tight and nobody will know the diff."

Puddin' then offered, in coarse language, an incentive for my cooperation. It sounded exciting, the way she said it, so I acquiesced to her terms and went to work on Puddin' in the manner indicated.

I had been endeavoring for several long minutes to give her some pleasure by the certain means she had suggested when Puddin' suddenly said, "I hate Newt Gingrich."

About two minutes later she said, "Hey. Who was the forgotten Beatle?" A minute after that she said a third thing, which was, "That's enough. Who taught you to do that?"

I sat up. "Nobody," I said.

"That's what I thought," she said.

"Pete Best," I said.

"What?" she said.

"He was the forgotten Beatle."

Puddin' tidied herself in a way that indicated our activities were over. "Okay, you got what you wanted," she said. "Fork over the hash."

"Please take a reasonable amount," I said. "You didn't seem to enjoy what I was doing. And now my back hurts."

Puddin' wasn't listening. She fished in her backpack and sighed. "After all that, I'm out of rolling papers. We need to use our wits, like on that TV show. Bow down for me."

I did what Puddin' said. She climbed on my shoulders and told me to get up so she could disable the smoke detector. I noticed again that her thighs smelled elegant, like a funeral parlor.

"Okay, let me down," she said.

I did.

"We need two butter knives and a plastic milk jug," she said.

"Where are we going to get that?"

"What about that little brick building on the side of the interstate? What is it, an office?"

"Yes."

"Well, they must have a break room or a kitchenette."

"My supervisor's over there," I said.

"I'm not asking for the world," said Puddin'.

"What's your plan?" I said.

"Have you heard of hot-knifing?"

"No."

"Then don't worry about my plan."

I returned to the main building and tried the handle, but the door was locked. There was a slot where you could slide your ID card and get in, but I didn't have an ID card, so I pressed a gray button I saw.

"Who's there?" said a voice.

"A maintenance worker," I said.

There was a pause during which I suppose I was scrutinized by unseen eyes, followed by a buzzing sound from within. I pulled on the door and it opened for me.

I could find no way of avoiding the supervisor's office. I breezed by. She was in there, with her blinds open, talking on the phone and laughing like it was the most ordinary day in the world. She didn't seem to see me. I went down the hall, looking in doors until I found the empty break room.

Over by the sink, someone had left the coffeemaker on with just a swallow of coffee left in the bottom of the pot. As a result, a hot black crust had formed. I turned off the coffeemaker as a courtesy, then began rooting through drawers for butter knives.

"You there!" someone shouted.

I cracked my head on the corner of a low-hanging cabinet. For a second all I could think about was the dizzying pain, then I turned to face the supervisor. My head smarted so much that there were tears in my eyes.

"Have you delivered the package?" she said.

"No ma'am."

"Then you better have a pretty good reason for abandoning your post."

"Oh, yes ma'am. I'm looking for an orange. Otherwise I might go into a swoon, as we discussed earlier."

"Didn't your friend bring you your medicine?"

"No ma'am, I've seen no one. I'm utterly alone."

She gave me a hard look that lasted forever and I thought the jig was up.

"Okay," she said. "Some people keep their lunches in the refrigerator, in paper bags. Find what you're looking for and get back where you belong. If you've screwed this up you'll be extremely sorry."

She split. I grabbed a handful of stainless steel butter knives—seven or eight—and made a beeline for the tollbooth.

Puddin' had a little fire going in the wastebasket, and a dirty old license plate laid flat across the top like a little table. It said "New Mexico, the Land of Enchantment" and it was just wide enough so that it didn't fall into the fire.

"I forgot the milk," I said, "but I got a load of knives."

"Forget the milk. Grab that bullhorn and hand it to me. I just need one knife now."

The tollbooth was getting smoky.

"This doesn't seem smart," I said. "How's the ventilation?"

"You worry too much."

"I almost got caught. She's on to us. We have to watch our step. I think the jig is up."

"Getting away with things is the norm," said Puddin'. She held the blade of her butter knife against the license plate, heating it. "Think about it. All you see on TV is when somebody gets caught at something that society has told us is wrong. But that's just one percent of the time. The other ninety-nine percent never get caught. People just don't care, or they don't know what they're seeing. It's a mathematical certainty that you'll never get caught at anything." She placed a small clump of hash onto the license plate. I stood there watching her, the megaphone in my hand. "I'm telling you, doing bad stuff is as safe as flying in an airplane. Come here."

Puddin' explained how to put the megaphone over the wastebasket, where to put my mouth, and when to take a deep breath and hold it.

The effect was like being shot in the chest with a hollow-tipped bullet of happiness. I can wholeheartedly recommend this method of consuming hash to any man, woman or child in the United States.

Puddin' grinned. "It's an instant high," she said. "I'm glad we didn't have the rolling papers. Now it's my turn."

Puddin' showed me how to smash the hash between the red-hot butter knife and the red-hot license plate, producing the wonderful smoke. She, too, breathed it in through the small end of the megaphone. We took several turns apiece and it was just the most pleasant morning you can think of. We got very wise and our heads opened up and that little tollbooth seemed like a universe of space.

Puddin' told me she could hear what the radios were playing in cars a hundred miles up the highway.

"What's so great about maple trees?" I said. "Let's start a business where we make syrup out of pine trees."

"Let's call Prince on my cell phone," she said. "No, let's go to his house and throw rocks through his windows until he comes outside. It's a three-day drive to Minneapolis from here. I'll call India and she'll come pick us up. We'll sell the rest of this hash on the way and then we'll have enough money to make your demo."

"What demo?" I said.

"You need some ambition," said Puddin'. "Prince can help you."

I became aware that a horn had been honking for some time. Puddin' started to say something about something but I held up my hand to shush her. We listened. It was amazing, because I realized that every honk of the horn was filled with literally millions of tones and overtones and undertones, some that the human ear was not meant to hear, but suddenly I could hear every layer. It was everything at once. It destroyed all the symphonies and concerti ever composed.

"A car horn is a perfect machine," I said. "I'm glad the band broke up."

I got to my feet and looked out the window. I realized that glass is just a slow-moving liquid. I saw the Volvo station wagon. There was a handsome man inside. He reminded me of Hamlet. Intense. Even from the tollbooth window I could tell that his eyelashes were really nice and luxurious.

"You're like the me that could have been, if everything had worked out good," I said. I suppose it was the hash talking.

Hamlet blinked at me and I started freaking out because I thought I could hear the soft sighs of his eyelashes.

"Let me get your hash," I said.

I looked down at the hash. A lot of it wasn't there anymore. The rest of it we had stepped in, and tracked all around the tollbooth, or sat in, or rolled around on. It was a terrible mess.

"One minute," I said.

I crouched down and asked Puddin' to put the hash back together again, the way she had promised. Then I popped back up.

"We're getting it ready right this second," I said. "Thank you for your patience."

I noticed that there was a long line of angry cars behind Hamlet. I noticed that he was getting something out of the glove compartment.

"How's it coming, Puddin'?" I said.

I looked behind me to see Puddin' crawling out the door of the booth.

I ran out after her.

We hauled butt across the paths of three other tollbooths and into the weeds on the wilder side of the highway. We pushed through a stand of scraggly saplings and went up the embankment to a chain link fence that neither of us was in the mood to climb. We kept following the fence, hoping it would end, but it never did.

"Stop," said Puddin'. "I know that Waffle House." She took out her cell phone and called India. "I'm on a hill overlooking the good Waffle House," she said. "You have to come get me. Bring wire cutters."

Soon I found myself lying in the back of India's van with her sheepdog. I looked into his warm black eyes and it was like I could see his ancestors.

"We should have brought that hash with us," said Puddin', who was riding up front. "I could really go for some more hash."

"Let's go to my stepmom's," said India. "We could drink her gin while she's off at spirituality training."

India is just seventeen, and I made it clear that I did not condone underage drinking. But I thanked her for her offer of hospitality and said that perhaps Puddin' and I would have a drink if she and her sheepdog didn't mind. Her sheepdog barked, which we humorously pretended was his way of voting "yes."

India's stepmom lives in a big mansion full of furniture. We went over and drank some gin in the garage. I suppose the alcoholic content of the gin caused me to become lax, because I noticed that at some point India had become drunken as well.

Puddin' and India got silly and started talking about a movie they loved, called *Hook*. They had a bunch of fun telling tales of how Dustin Hoffman would eat a head of garlic before every scene just to get a certain reaction from his co-stars, in a method acting sense. They giggled and squawked about it until I could tell what they were really signaling to each other: that I had bad breath. Why not just come out and say it instead of making an inside joke? It got on my nerves. I didn't tell them I was on to them but I left them snickering and noticed it was dark outside.

My car was back at the tollbooth place so I walked home, about four miles. I live with my parents in a subdivision called King Arthur Courts. I guess I got turned around a few times. Everything in a subdivision looks the same. That's why Puddin' hates America. When I finally made it home I noted with some curiosity that there were several plates broken on the kitchen floor. I guess there were some other irregularities as well, which I somehow overlooked at the time. I went back in my parents' bedroom and got on the internet.

I Googled myself, which is a little tradition I have. As usual, there was an archival list that mentioned me in conjunction with my old high school's lacrosse team. This always struck me as hilarious because I never was on the lacrosse team. The supposedly infallible internet is not so infallible after all.

Believe it or not, there is a man with the same name as mine who runs a petting zoo in White Knob, Idaho. I always enjoy visiting the petting zoo's web site and clicking on "Recent News." Usually there is no recent news. Once I sent the other "me" an email about our coincidental similarity of names, but I have never heard back from him. It occurred to me that he might even be dead.

I was amusing myself in this fashion when I heard the sounds of my father creeping through the house.

"Hello? Hello?" he was saying. "Junior, is that you?"

I greeted him in the hallway.

My father is a portly man with a big, fine head of bushy gray hair. He is around sixty years of age or so, I believe.

"Where's Mom?" I said.

"She's at the hospital. Two men visited us tonight. They said you owed them fifteen thousand dollars. When we expressed our astonishment, they hit me in the breadbasket five times, knocking the wind out of me. They also twisted my arm behind my back, harshly. These same gentlemen gave your mother two black eyes and kicked her down the front steps. She has a concussion and perhaps some other problems, perhaps a broken back. She's being kept overnight for observation."

"Oh my goodness," I said.

"I hate to think you've gotten mixed up with these kind of men," said my father.

"Fifteen thousand dollars doesn't sound right," I said. "I think someone is trying to pull my leg."

"Maybe it was fifteen hundred. They broke my false teeth," said my father. "This is my spare set, and they don't fit me right."

"They should deduct two hundred dollars right off the top," I said. "I never received my two hundred dollars. I'm going to make Mom a get-well card using PhotoShop. I'm getting pretty good at it."

"That sounds thoughtful," said my father.

"That means I'm going to be in your bedroom for awhile," I said. "Undisturbed."

"Be my guest. I can't sleep anyway," he said. "I'm too worked up."

"Watch some TV," I suggested.

"They urinated on the surge protector and now the TV doesn't work anymore," he replied.

I then left my father to his own devices. Once I had secured my parents' bedroom door I looked up India's MySpace page and masturbated to relieve myself of the stress. Afterward I sent an email to Laura Bush via the White House web site, briefly outlining the events of the day, which is a hobby of mine.

COURAGEOUS BLAST:
THE LEGACY OF AMERICA'S MOST RADICAL GUM

CONRAD HATCHER, *Project Manager*:
Look. We all knew we had something awesome. The suits didn't know. They were all like, "Whoa!" They were like, "Dude!" I didn't care what they said. I was all up in Wayne Goodwin's face. I was all like, "Dude, we're going to make a gum that's like, radical and everything?" And he was all like, "Whatever."

WAYNE GOODWIN, *VP—Marketing*:
I suppose I had some misgivings of a practical nature. But I think you will find that overall there hasn't been a more enthusiastic supporter of the gum, in terms of letting those guys explore, you know, and find their level. I sensed from the very beginning that we were on to something quite important here. The undiscovered country, if you will. Uncharted waters. Here there be monsters. Bracing, exciting stuff. Danger, Will Robinson! Wonderful stuff. Fearless.

BRAVO JONES, *Logo Designer*:
Conrad is a risk taker. I will give him that. We've had our differences, as is well documented. But I like to give credit where credit is due. It's something I do naturally. I'm a truth teller. A lot of times that freaks people out. I always say, "Look, I'm just being honest." You know, "You're fat, you're a pig," or whatever. My attitude is, take it or leave

it. But don't put me down for telling it like it is. For example, at the first meeting with Conrad I say, "Hey, what's the name of this gum?" Because at that time the gum had no name. I mean I can do a lot of things, and do them fantastically well, but I'm not a miracle worker! Am I? Maybe I am. Otherwise I honestly believe there would have been a gum in the stores with no name on it. And that would have blown people's minds. Not in a good way.

CONRAD HATCHER:

It sounds funny, but it's really not. I was, like, looking at the package and all of a sudden I was like, "Hey." You know what I mean? I was like, "What's *in* there?" I was trying to get inside the customer's head or whatever. So I was like, "What's *in* this package of gum, dude?" And then I was like, "I don't know, but it better be gum." Like I was answering my own self. Weird. Like I was having two parts of the same conversation, but there's only like one of me there. So I was just like, *It Better Be Gum.*

WAYNE GOODWIN:

What we were doing with It Better Be Gum was throwing caution to the wind. I mean, why not? It seems easy in retrospect, but at the time it was a truly courageous vision. There's a lot of talk right now about courage and whatnot, but whenever I'm pressed for a definition I just say, take a look at It Better Be Gum. Try to place yourself in what was really a gum vacuum at that time, and imagine It Better Be Gum bursting forth like some sort of courageous blast of dynamite. That's courage. To create something out of nothing. Which is what we do every day in this business. And I fully credit Conrad with that. He was the one with the forethought to say, "Who cares if it's a chewing gum or a bubble gum?" You know. "We're not going to tell people. We're not going to give them that crutch. Let them decide for themselves whether to chew it or blow it. And hey, maybe we can make it where they can swallow it." Because before that, you know, no one was allowed to swallow gum. That's a discredited way of thinking now, and yes, I suppose Conrad is principally responsible for that, for what I would call a *sea change* in the way Americans engage with gum as a recreational snack.

STANLEY BOUNCE, *Gum Aficionado*:

They test marketed It Better Be Gum in Texarkana. I don't know where else. All I know is, me and my friends were the only people putting it in our mouths. Like, "I dare you to put this in your mouth!" Because after you spit it out there was still like this greasy feeling and this weird bitter taste. And when I went number two it *burned*! But I didn't associate that with It Better Be Gum. I just thought there was something wrong with me. Then my friend Glen was in the bathroom for like, forever, and I was like, "What's up?" And he was like, "Every time I chew this gum I get like, the runs." And I was like, cool.

SARA SPOONER, *The "It Better Be Gum Girl"*:

The gorilla in the commercial was super sweet! He would sit in the corner and go "Uh, uh, uh!" I think he was trying to talk to me! That was super sweet. There wasn't a mouth on the mask where the gorilla could talk out of, so it just sounded like "Uh, uh, uh!" to me. But he acted super sweet. He waved to me and everything. Like, "How are you?" Or, "Good morning, Sara!" But he didn't use words to express it. Just "Uh, uh, uh!" It made me feel bright and cheerful. That was sad when he died.

CONRAD HATCHER:

When the monkey man died I was like, "Whoa!" I was like, "Heavy, dude." I was like, "What the fuck?" I was like, "Who's going to be the monkey man now?"

STANLEY BOUNCE:

I'll never forget the first It Better Be Gum commercial. I had all my homies with me because you know, this was a gum that only we knew about. So we just crouched around the television, there was about fifteen of us and my Mom made fudge. Plus we were all chewing It Better Be Gum. It was kind of a bummer because everybody in the whole world was going to know about our secret thing. But there was like a definite party atmosphere. And when that monkey came out and started dancing his ass off, that sealed the deal, bro! That was the funniest damn monkey I ever saw. He was going [demonstrates monkey movements]. It was like the monkey was saying, "Back off, parents! You can't understand this gum!" And the sexy girl was like, "That's right!" But they said it through their motions of dancing. Glen literally went in his pants he was laughing so hard. He couldn't get in the bathroom either because somebody else was in there with the runs. That was the greatest night of my life.

WAYNE GOODWIN:

I really felt that Chunkafella, the It Better Be Gum Monkey, was an almost holy character, like a Hindu god or something. And when that guy died, the guy who usually put on the gorilla suit, the whole *weltzschmertz* changed. It was like the spiritual center had just crumbled somehow. You could feel it. Of course, it was impossible to tell him apart from the next guy who put on the gorilla suit—impossible on a literal level, because, you know, it's some guy in a gorilla suit—but on a subliminal level it broke my heart.

CONRAD HATCHER:

They kept making me think there would be Choco-Grape It Better Be Gum with Super Flavor Bombs and everything, and I was like, stoked. And then it would be like, "Sorry, Dude, I changed my mind. The juice runoff from your gum totally eats people's stomach lining for some reason." Whatever. At first I was all, "Whoa." Now I'm like, "Whatever." I guess America's not ready for something that's going to eat their precious stomach lining. You know, okay, that's your problem, not mine. I'm glad I had the experience. It made me think about my thoughts as a human being or some shit. Anyway I got a lot of other stuff I'm doing right now. Like this gum called Project Blue. It's going to totally turn your mouth and teeth and everything blue and the stain won't ever come out. America is going to be like, "Dude!" And I'm going to be like, "Whatever, America."

THE TRAIN GOING BACK

A man like a big egg sat down and dunked a tea bag.

"This is my tea bag," he said. "This is a tea bag I brought from home. You think the water's free? Oh sure, the water's free. The water's free but the cup'll cost you. That's some scam they have going. The guy tells me the water's free but if I want a cup to put it in, that's another story."

The young man didn't know what to say.

"I know what," the egg man said. "I should bring my own cup next time. I ought to make a note of that."

He whipped out a pad.

"Bring...own...cup."

He snapped it shut.

"I'm a travel writer," he said. "I have two weekly columns in _____." (He named a certain city.) "A lot of these guys have been doing it fifteen, twenty years and they can't get a column. I have two."

"Man."

"I'm just lucky, I guess. I try to give the reader an image, you know? Anybody can say, go here, this restaurant has good food. I try to be a little more enticing. Last week I was in [another city] at this place called The Coachman's Inn, and the girl gets wind I'm a travel writer so she asks me if I'm going to mention the place. I tell her, 'I'm not just going to mention it, I'm going to make people want to come here.' So what do I write? The soup's good? The Coachman's Inn has a nice selection of desserts? No, it's 'a spicy vegetable soup with a flavor that can only be described as more, more, more. And don't leave without trying the blackberry cobbler, served in a rich, creamery sauce.' See?"

The young man said he saw. The travel writer seemed to feel a warm connection, perhaps something to do with the great book the boy was holding. Men of literature! Men who appreciated things! Men of the world. But he didn't say it outright. He just talked some more about how great he was and how great it was to be a travel writer. He talked and talked and finally he paused long enough for the boy to excuse himself.

The boy stood in the restroom, smelling the soiled cake of air freshener and shaking with the train. He put gray water on his face and looked in the mirror. You can imagine what he saw.

When the boy came back, the travel writer had gone. The boy had failed him somehow. He sat down and looked out the window again.

The things going by stung his heart. A stop sign. Deep orange weeds, golden as oranges. Murky, opaline water in ditches. Cherry-colored and pink and turquoise clothes blowing on a line.

Where had he gotten opaline? Probably from the supposedly great book she had given him and commanded him to read.

Cherry-colored? Try plain old red. Some sad red rags and an old woman's enormous yellowed bra.

Litter. Burned trees. Graveyards. Appliance stores. An abandoned gas station. A rusted washing machine.

How about the time a moth had flown into her cleavage? That was the day they met.

He remembered picking beans in his good shoes and pants. She filled an old fishing hat full of water and pressed it down on his head.

He remembered riding on the back of her motorcycle, French

bread in a grocery bag flapping against his leg.

A baseball game on the radio.

Each thing that had happened was a little thing. It was normal life. But everything had taken on special properties, like objects through the window of a train. The combination of little normal things had turned into a large unnameable thing and made him fall in love.

It was dinnertime and the lounge car had begun to empty. He looked out the window.

More things went by. Power poles. Flowers. Cows in a field. The sky turned lemony at the bottom and a painful watercolor blue at the top. Pretty soon it was dark, and between the lit cities it was very dark.

ROGER HILL

Everybody smokes cigars now. Famous people. There are magazines about it. Women smoke cigars. It doesn't matter. Meg won't let me have one in the house.

It was a Sunday afternoon before Christmas, unseasonably warm. I had just settled into the porch swing and lit up when I saw my next-door neighbor Roger Hill standing in his yard like a statue, staring across the street. His fists were clenched by his sides.

I knew what he was looking at: the nasty army-barracks green of the house opposite his. It was a black eye for the whole neighborhood but especially bothered Roger, who had to confront it every day from his breakfast table.

I must tell you that we live in an exceptionally fine neighborhood. Halfway down the street it turns into a place where blacks live in horrible conditions, I won't mince words. What people don't understand is that they don't want to come over here any more than we want to go over there. We get along just fine thank you and nobody's complaining.

Of course a lot of the money has moved west to the suburbs but those people are just chicken to live near the blacks—incredible in this day and age!—and there is a nucleus of the younger set who prefer, like Meg and myself, to stay close to downtown and work toward gentrification rather than cowering in the shadow of those damn shopping malls.

We're like pioneers. The homes in which we live were built a hundred years ago or more, when the city was a rich and bejeweled center of enlightenment, and a couple are even older, from when cotton was still king. There is a monthly award for the most attractive yard, and some of the homes are open for tours during a long weekend every spring.

Because we live in an official historic district, we are required by the city to sign a pledge that we will treat our property in certain ways. One of the most important is that each house must be painted in a shade—honeysuckle, mint julep, stardust, johnny reb gray, and so on—exactly consistent with the decorating practices of antebellum days. The city has gone to a lot of trouble to scientifically reproduce an abundant registry of authentic colors, but apparently none of them had been good enough for the new fellow across the street.

I walked over to commiserate with Roger.

"Look at that," he said. "I've called the city three times, and nothing. And I've been watching. Hell, I spent half the day yesterday standing at the window, waiting for a city car to pull up, and all I saw was that damn woman picking up sticks in the yard, which was not a pretty sight when she bent over, let me tell you. He probably just waved some cash in their faces, that's all, that's probably how he got the house to begin with. The only place you'll find a color like that is if you go down to south Broad Street and look at a row of n———-r houses."

I guess it was bad of me, but I didn't object to his language at the time because he was so obviously upset. And anyway there is no denying the pitiful state of those houses on Broad Street. Hell, that's just a simple fact, and if that makes me a racist, well lock me up. Personally, I would never use the word that Roger used, but you can't say anything true nowadays because of this political correctness they have going around.

Roger reached down and pulled up a clump of weeds.

"I'm letting the whole place go to pot. Used to be there was nothing I liked better than getting out in the yard, puttering around, do a little gardening, a little landscaping. Sally would say, 'Why don't you just hire a yard man?' and I'm going, 'Oh, no, honey, I *enjoy* doing this.' Well shit. Now I don't even care. You look at that shit across the street and you think, 'What's the point?' Picking up sticks in the yard. God! Have you *seen* that woman? She's as big as a barn and she wears halter tops. She looks like a piece of white trash fresh from the trailer park."

"They're not married is what I hear," I told him.

"That's perfect."

Roger dropped the weeds and dusted off his hands. He headed back for his house. The door slammed behind him. I didn't think much of it at the time. He had a right to be upset. I finished my cigar and went inside.

That evening there were four or five police cars parked on the street and in Roger's yard. I was already down the steps to check it out and Meg was standing in the doorway when a man came up the walk to meet me. He showed me his badge and asked if we had heard anything unusual in the past hour or so.

I looked back at Meg. "We've been watching television," she said, sounding shaky. Her arms were crossed tight.

"What happened?" I asked.

What had happened was that Roger Hill had shot and killed his wife and himself.

It didn't seem like any fun to watch HBO after that. We went upstairs and sat on our bed in the dark. Periodically, one of us would get up and peek through the blinds. Once, Meg stood there a long time and I finally said, "What?"

She whispered, "They're bringing them out."

By the time I got to the window, they were shutting the ambulance door.

I guess I made a disappointed noise. Actually, what I said was, "Shoot."

Meg looked at me.

The phone rang. Meg said to let the voice mail pick it up. It rang again. It kept ringing. Meg turned off the ringer, and our cell phones, and everything. I had the urge to chew the fat with some of the other key people on the block. Meg wanted quality time instead. She sat on the bed again. I looked out the window.

"Everybody's down there," I said. "Nobody's running them off."

"Quality time," said Meg. So nothing happened. That's what quality time is.

The news had the whole story by ten. They reported that Roger and Sally had been in the middle of a difficult divorce. The children were in Atlanta on a visit with Roger's parents. Roger had called the elder Mr. Hill and told him something like, "I've just shot Sally and now I'm going to shoot myself."

Well, the neighborhood was in shock. No one had an inkling that Roger and Sally were getting a divorce.

We all chipped in to take care of Roger's lawn. The new fellow across the street even waddled over once and offered to help but we told him no thanks, we had it under control.

*

Christmas came up fast. We were in the family room, where the tree was. Charlotte and Nathan had their gifts spread all over the floor. Nathan spent most of the time putting together his microscope and taking it apart again. He is an incredibly intelligent six-year-old who is enrolled in a school for the gifted. Charlotte, seven, is not too bright.

Also present were Meg's parents, down from Hilton Head, as well as Meg's brother Chip, who is a prominent gynecologist up in Charleston. Chip brought his teenage son Josh, of whom he has full custody because his ex-wife is crazy. Josh, as I understand it, is a recovered or recovering drug addict.

Meg sipped a g-and-t and told how Roger had gotten all the honeysuckle out of a rosebush for her. "He was so thoughtful. I can't imagine him doing something like that—the, you know, violence."

"Well, you know what Kafka said," Chip told her. "People either die of boredom or shoot themselves out of curiosity. Or wait a minute. Was that Kierkegaard? One of those K people, anyway. They're all depressing." He laughed.

"I wish you wouldn't joke about it," Meg said.

Chip got up for more bourbon. He waved Meg off. Josh, who had been propped in the doorway with his mouth clamped shut all afternoon, said, "It's like corn."

"Good God Almighty, a voice from the grave!" Meg's father said.

"What was that, son?" Chip asked, pouring.

"Remember that band Korn? They like start with a K, and they're like all angry and energetic and stuff like you're talking about."

"That's great, Dumbo. I liked it better when you were doing your Helen Keller act." Chip went over to the loveseat where Meg was sitting, and perched on the arm.

"Look, honey. You think I'm cruel because I joke about a terrible thing. You must understand that once we reach a certain point of sophistication that's the way we deal with life. You've heard the business about laughing so you don't cry and blah blah blah? It's like *South Park*."

"Helen Keller wasn't depressing and she starts with a K," said Josh. "She was like a hero or whatever."

"Oh yeah," said Chip. "Some blind girl smashing into everything and making those weird noises—ahwah yahyah yah. *That's* not depressing at all. Right. Can't you just imagine her crapping on herself?"

"Oh my goodness, Chip," said Meg.

"I'm using that as an example of spoofing. Nothing should be off limits. They have another one on the comedy channel about this big he-man superhero and all these other comic-book characters, like Betty Boop. And one time the he-man dresses up like a girl and gets gang-raped. Aw, don't you get it? It's a spoof on Jodie Foster, all those movies she used to make about boo hoo hoo, I got raped. I swear, sometimes I think I've got more of a young spirit about me than this sensitive little genius over here. What's the matter, genius, are you in love with Jodie Foster? Sorry I made fun of your girlfriend." Chip put this last zinger to Josh.

Josh looked away in a supposedly cool fashion, but I think everyone could tell he had been bested. Chip turned his attention back to Meg.

"I'll give you an example. When I was interning, these doctors who bossed us around, they had code words for everything. 'Gomer' was a big one. 'Gomer.' Do you know what that is?"

We all said no.

"It's an acronym. It stands for Get-Out-of-My-Emergency-Room, and it refers to the pathetic old geezers who tend to clutter up the place when they should really just go home and die. Now Gomers are divided into two categories: the Os and the Qs. Os are the ones who are so far gone that their mouths just hang open. That's the O." He demonstrated, tilting back his head and letting his jaw drop so that his mouth formed a round hole.

"And here's a Q." He did the same thing, except that he let his tongue dangle out.

Josh didn't laugh, but the rest of us did, including Charlotte.

"They're even worse," Chip said, talking about the Qs. "Within a week we realized there was nothing we could do to help them, they were just getting in the way. We were hollering 'Gomer' right along with everybody else. And this is years before *South Park*."

"That's real funny," said Josh. "Don't you think you might have hurt those old people's feelings or whatever, talking about them like that?"

"Believe me, son, they were beyond any conception of what we were saying."

"You don't know that for sure."

"Yes, I'm afraid I do."

"It's impossible to know for sure what's going on in somebody else's mind."

"Oh, what a wonderful insight. Well, you're mistaken, son. That schoolyard crap about who really knows what a dog is thinking and so on is bullshit. And I'll tell you something else. When you've got children coming in with head trauma, gunshot wounds..."

"That's not exactly where you stick your fingers now, is it?" said Josh.

Chip jumped up and screamed, "*I am a doctor!*" His drink went everywhere.

Josh said big deal and left. The front door slammed.

"Well, Happy Birthday, Little Lord Jesus," said Meg's father. I could see Josh through the bay window, standing on the porch, lighting a cigarette.

"Shit, Meg, don't worry about your carpet. Most of it's on my pants." Chip slurped the bourbon off his fingers and went back to the bar. "You know why an alcoholic gynecologist is best, don't you?"

He started to make a crude joke but Meg cut him off. "Chip! Nathan is very impressionable."

"No I'm not," Nathan said. We adults laughed because you don't expect a normal six-year-old to say something like that. "I like it when

Uncle Chip tells stories. Do you want to hear a story I know?"

"Yes by God we do!" said Meg's father. He patted his knee and Nathan came over and sat on it.

"Okay. It's like this. There was this little boy and his parents died and he had to live in a cage."

"Lord have mercy!" said Meg's mother.

"It's true, too," said Nathan. "It's a real story of real life. One day the little boy got out of the cage and he went to live in the woods like a bear. One day some nice people found him and they adopted him and took him to live with them. They had a nice house and they already had a little girl.

"But the little boy was too crazy to live in a regular house. He just ran around like a nut and broke everything so they had to lock him up in the attic.

"Okay, and the little girl's room was right under the attic and every night she heard a scritch-scritch-scratch and her parents told her it was rats. One night it got so loud that she went up the stairs and peeked through a crack in the door and there was the little boy, skinny as a skeleton, and he was taking his long fingernails and making a scritch-scritch-scratch on the floor.

"The little girl felt so sorry for him that she went to the kitchen and fixed a great big picnic basket of all the food she could find.

"The next morning her parents went to get her up for school and there was nobody in her bed. They looked all over the house and then they looked in the attic. There was the little boy scrunched up in the corner eating something. And there was the picnic basket and they looked in it and all it had in it was bones. That was the little girl's bones." Nathan shrugged and grinned. "He ate her up!"

"Merciful heavens!" said Meg's mother. Chip let out a good long laugh.

"Do you want to give your sister a nightmare?" said Meg.

Charlotte had tears in her eyes and a finger up her nose. What a mess. Sometimes I just don't know.

Meg went overboard and sent Nathan to his room. We could hear him up there, crying and breaking stuff. Before long it seemed like everybody was crying about something. "Hey, Meg, what's eating you?" said Chip. "Get it?"

The next day everybody felt like crap. The sound of working woke us up. Who works the day after Christmas?

It was a bunch of blacks. They were climbing all over that house across from the Hill place, repainting.

Gosh, if only Roger could have held out for a few months. It looks like magnolia.

YOUR BODY IS CHANGING

1

Henry and his mother returned home from Wednesday-night prayer meeting to find an enormous owl eating sausage biscuits out of a torn sack on the kitchen counter. When they walked in the door, the owl turned its head all the way around on its neck and looked over at them just as calm as could be, and it was holding a biscuit in one set of talons like a man eating half a sandwich.

"Uncle Lipton!" hollered Henry's mom. Those were Uncle Lipton's favorite biscuits, but Uncle Lipton was nowhere to be seen.

The owl knocked a whole slew of stuff off the counter as it craned and shook its broad wings. Henry's mom went for the broom. She tried to tell Henry what to do but he became confused and ran screaming down the hall.

The owl took off after him, emitting a constant stream of silky yellow defecation, but the short and narrow hallway did not accommodate its wingspan. It lost control, destroyed a row of family photographs, and barreled into Henry's back. Henry fell on his chin, splitting the tip of his tongue down the middle.

Henry rolled over to see the owl careen into the small, pale bathroom. It tore off the shower curtain and, wrapped and blinded, flew into the mirror on the medicine chest, smashing it into diamonds.

Henry scrambled up and shut the door.

"What have you done?" said Henry's mother.

"Now it can't get out," said Henry.

"But we *want* it to get out," said Henry's mother.

Henry spat a great bit of blood onto the floor.

They found Uncle Lipton curled up in a cabinet under the kitchen sink, next to the bug spray and Mr. Clean. His eyes wouldn't open all the way and he was humming a tune.

2

Just a few days earlier everything had been like normal. The chapel smelled like furniture polish. If Henry squinted, Amy Middleton from the eleventh grade looked like Polly Finch from behind, the American hero who had been exploded in a methamphetamine lab as part of the war on terrorism.

The devil slapped a picture of Laura Prepon into Henry's head to get him off track so he couldn't concentrate on the Word of the Lord.

Laura Prepon, the actress who portrayed the redheaded girl on *That '70s Show*, had gone on Conan O'Brien to talk about shooting a movie in Alabama. When she said Alabama something happened in Henry's pants. Where in Alabama? Was she coming back? Why was the world keeping them apart? Oh, Laura Prepon, you have the wide enticing face of a beauteous harlot. You have a vulva like a velvet boat.

It was eye-opening to be in Alabama. It was educational to find out that people could be so different, said Laura Prepon. One person from Alabama had tried to fashion a welcome sign for her as a gesture of goodwill, but this Alabama person did not go about his task properly. The sign was crudely constructed, which gave Laura Prepon a window into Alabama's soul, as she explained to Conan O'Brien. Alabama people did not know how to make neat, orderly signs, unlike the rest of the country. Another creepy person from Alabama actually tried to touch her in a coffee shop. Laura Prepon did not know how she managed to stay in Alabama for almost two weeks.

Henry wished that one day he would see Laura Prepon walking through a restaurant with everyone paying attention to her because she was a star of liberal Hollywood. Then he would stick out his foot real casual and trip her, not so she'd get hurt but just embarrassed and everybody would laugh at her so she would know what it felt like. Then he would help her up and reassure her that people are people wherever you go. "For man looketh on the outward appearance, but the Lord looketh on the heart." Then he would insert his penis into her naked vagina and make a baby, her white legs wrapped all the way around him, legs just about as white as raw chicken legs.

But that was not the way he thought of Polly Finch. He wanted to hug Polly Finch respectfully and tell her everything was okay and lick the inside of her mouth with his tongue.

Poor Polly Finch! Minding her own business! And then she had spotted the innocent Chinese baby walking toward the methamphetamine lab in Upstate New York. Just as she tossed the baby out of the way into a soft bush everything blew up. Now she was paralyzed from the neck down and also from the neck up, and mercifully asleep in a coma, but they thought she could understand what people were saying. One time somebody had said something sad about Jesus and a tear had trickled out of her paralyzed eye! Another time the President had called her on the telephone and told her that it turned out those methamphetamine people had been sending money overseas for terrorism and he thanked her on behalf of the United States for bringing everything out in the clear sunshine of truth, and while he was saying it one side of her paralyzed mouth went up in a smile. There were several witnesses! She was the Miracle Girl of Upstate New York and a warning to terrorists

of all stripes that you can't get the American people down. There was
that one home video where she was drinking punch in the weeks before
the tragedy, they showed it on the news every night and she stuck out
her tongue and it was all red, bright red, as red as Kool-Aid! It was a
famous image that had turned her into America's favorite paralyzed
sweetheart and caused Henry to fall in love, even though she was nineteen years old and already out of high school and paralyzed all over.

Henry remembered that he was in the chapel, looking at the back
of Amy Middleton's neck, so much like Polly Finch's neck, and the
whitish hairs creeping up it, shaped like an arrow, darkening as they
climbed. If you lifted up Polly Finch's long hair that smelled like apple
shampoo to give her her special hospital bath you would see something
like that underneath. Or if her beautiful hair was all bunched up in her
special headgear that she wore for paralysis. He'd like to blow on the
back of Amy Middleton's neck and watch the hairs wave like a pasture
of tall grass. All at once his lips got so dry he could feel them cracking.
One time Amy Middleton had walked by him after softball in her red
shorts and he had caught a waft of something that smelled like a hot
ironing board and made him dizzy.

These were wrong thoughts for chapel. What if Henry was a
sociopath, like on A&E? Normal on the outside but tortured by wrong
thoughts. What about voices in your head? Wasn't a thought just a
voice in your head? Sociopath was really just a politically correct way
to say "the devil." Henry shook his head to rattle the wrong thoughts
loose. It worked. The evangelist was saying:

"One evening at a state fair I came into my employer's luxurious
trailer and found him crying his eyes out. Yes, this very same man with
the world at his feet! I was stunned and flabbergasted. In my estimation
at the time, he was infinitely my superior. I could not imagine why a
person of such lofty attainments would ever need to shed a tear, and I

told him as much, for we were as close as brothers in our way. This man gestured wearily between his wrenching sobs at his thousand-dollar monkey and his empty liquor bottles and the crumpled pornography that littered the filthy hole he called his home. 'Sam,' he said to me, 'all of this means nothing. I believe it is time for us to get right with the Lord.' And the name of that man was…Neil Sedaka. Who amongst you is familiar with Neil Sedaka?"

No one was familiar with Neil Sedaka.

"Calendar Girl?" said the evangelist. "Breaking Up Is Hard to Do?"

He was an old man with deep red wrinkles and blinding white needles of hair and nobody knew what he was talking about.

There was a time before the evangelist had been saved when he partook of mind-blowing drugs and toured with a band. They had "crashed" at a Catholic's house because there was nowhere else to stay. The evangelist had sprung awake in the dead of night with two searing pinholes of pain in his back. Well, it turned out there was a crucifix attached to the wall and the bloody tortured Christ was boring into the evangelist's back with little lasers coming out of the scrunched-up pain-filled eyes in His twisted face.

That was an interesting story. It made Henry feel weird and excited, like when the man with the motorcycle had jumped over trash-cans for the Lord or when the fat man had lain there with cinderblocks on his stomach and somebody had smashed them with a sledgehammer for the Lord, and the fat man got up and he was perfectly fine. That was in the gym.

The evangelist pointed out that the cross in the chapel was bare.

Real Christians worshipped the triumphant Christ no cross could hold, whose body was glorified, resurrected and incorruptible, but Catholics had a perversion that bade them concentrate on fleshly things and worship graven images. They whipped themselves with whips and slept in coffins and all they cared about was the sick, dying human carcass that the Lord had discarded like the trash it was.

The evangelist said everybody should bring something to the fifty-yard line to burn on Friday. Rosaries, crucifixes, pocket-sized idols of the Virgin Mary, whatever was Catholic that you could get your hands on. One time he had burned some junk like that and you could hear the demons screaming as they spewed out of the fire, but he couldn't promise anything.

3

Henry Gill didn't sleep much. He was fourteen—a thin, worried boy with a wet-looking bowl of black hair and countless eruptions on his sweet, horrible face. He had big blue circles around his eyes, skin the color of skim milk, and a big soft lump on the left side of his chest.

They had thought at first it might be cancer but the doctors tested him out and discovered that his hormones had gone crazy. Henry had too much estrogen. It made the doctor laugh for some reason and then he stopped laughing and got serious.

"You are at a confusing age. I can assure you, however, that you are not going to grow a breast like a young lady. But please come back and see me if you do. Or seriously, if it gets any larger or becomes discolored or tender to the touch. My feeling is, it will eventually take care of itself."

But so far it hadn't.

Henry got free tuition to the Christian school because of his hardships. He lived with his mother and her uncle, an angry photographer who wore a bathrobe all day. Changes in photography trends and a series of near-fatal aneurysms had ruined Uncle Lipton's life and personality. He only came out of his room—it used to be the sewing room until he moved in—to drive his dying car to Hardee's for a sack of sausage biscuits and a dozen packs of mustard. It was all he would eat. He wouldn't drink anything.

4

It came out that before her tragedy Polly Finch had supposedly let some army boys take pictures of her showing her chest, also with her jeans unzipped and "touching herself." Also wearing a blue thong.

Henry hated the elite liberal media so much. They just had to ruin everything. Why didn't his pants realize the reports were unconfirmed? The devil kept popping pictures in his head of Polly Finch shivering and shirtless, smiling at him, with twin pink bull's-eyes on her chest and the chilly golden flesh of a nectarine.

He got out his book, the book his grandmother had given him, *Your Body Is Changing: A Christian Teen's Guide to Sexuality.* It was the greatest book ever. It smelled like cedar because he kept it at the bottom of his sock drawer. He wanted to understand his feelings.

Later that night Henry fell asleep in front of the TV. He was awakened when Jesus sat on the arm of the couch. Henry was surprised to learn that Jesus looked a lot like Luke, the scruffy diner-owner on *Gilmore Girls*, a show Henry watched on cable every day after school.

"Hello, Henry, there's someone I'd like you to meet," said Jesus.

Henry looked in the doorway and saw a girl floating there, wearing a thin robe, bathed in orange light.

"Is that Polly Finch?" said Henry.

"Yes," said Jesus. "You sure are smart." He rubbed Henry's head.

"Look, I've come out of my body," said Polly Finch. "I need you to put me back in."

"Okay," said Henry.

"Thanks, Henry," said Jesus. "I knew I could count on you."

"I don't understand what I'm supposed to do," said Henry.

Jesus started to mumble, and Henry was afraid to ask Him to speak up.

All this occurred the day before the owl got in and gave Uncle Lipton his famous aneurysm.

5

Uncle Lipton became a kind of celebrity within hours of being rolled into the emergency room. The X-rays showed a gigantic aneurysm, the biggest one yet for Uncle Lipton, maybe the biggest one ever for anybody. Maybe it wasn't even an aneurysm. Maybe it was a new discovery. Doctors the world over wanted to study him. There was this one doctor in London, England, who said, Come on over, the ticket's on me! There wasn't a moment to lose.

Everybody said this was the man to see. If he couldn't fix Uncle Lipton nobody could.

One doctor told Henry not to eat solids for awhile and gave him some gel for his tongue, which had been injured during the problem with the owl. The gel turned Henry's whole head numb and cozy. All of a sudden he was on a helicopter pad on top of the hospital and his mother was telling him goodbye.

"Are you sure you're going to be okay while I'm gone to London, England?"

"Yes ma'am."

"Call Ruth Ann, okay? She'll take care of you. Tell her I'm sorry this is so sudden."

A scientist pointed at his watch.

Henry's mother got into the helicopter with Uncle Lipton. The blades sliced the sky, faster and faster, and everyone had to go back inside the hospital. Henry's mother told him something, but he couldn't hear what.

6

Henry called animal control from a pay phone in the lobby and told them, "I got a sick owl in my house."

After that, he took off walking. He walked through the glass doors and the vestibule and another set of glass doors and across the wide parking lot into the decorative trees and he just kept walking.

November in Alabama had been until that point as hot as a furnace but the Lord saw fit to put a tribulation in Henry's path. The Lord found Henry in nothing but his good blue pants and a white T-shirt spotted with blood from his broken tongue and his hard black school shoes with no socks (Henry must have left the socks, along with his church shirt, in the scooped seat of the doctor's plastic chair), and He blew a cold front through the state with whipping winds.

It was like Henry understood free will for the first time. You don't have to call Ruth Ann. You don't have to go home. It's cold, but you can stay out in the cold. You can shoplift, theoretically. You can try to buy alcohol. You can undo your pants. You can pee on somebody's flowerbed. You can do bad things because your mother isn't around. Then, when you heed the Lord instead, that's the only time it really counts.

Henry was in a wooded area, to which the hospital's landscaping had subtly given way, when he remembered a video about devil worshippers they had watched in Social Studies. A repentant devil worshipper with long sideburns had explained that when you first try to sell your soul to the devil all nature goes against you. Rabbits and frogs and all kinds of animals come out of the woods and speak in human tongues and beg you not to do what you intend. Three times you have to turn them away, then they throw in the towel. Next thing you know, the devil comes out and gives you a bag with something awful in it.

What did Jesus want from Henry? Something about helping Polly Finch, or seeing her in person, in her coma pajamas, or praying over her so her legs started kicking, or marrying her, or appearing with her on the cover of a magazine at the drugstore where everybody could see it. And now, thanks to free will, everybody's dream could come true.

The Lord guided Henry through the trees and onto a golf course, a kind of place where Henry had never been in real life. He crossed the sleepy hills, the still waters, the sandy places, until he witnessed something like a long fat serpent writhing on the ground. Henry squatted in a stand of shrubbery and peeked at the snaky thing, which turned out to be two people trying to fornicate in a sleeping bag.

"Uh, uh, uh," they said.

From what little he could tell it was just the way Henry had imagined it.

There were some sounds of aggravation and then a brief silence.

"It's cold, baby. I'm not getting any blood to it."

"I knew this was a mistake."

The sound of weeping. The whoremonger had made the woman cry. No—it was the *man* crying! A crying man!

"Let me try again. I promise I can do it."

"You had your big chance, junior. I'll tell you one thing. You *will* walk me back to the dorm. And you're not coming in for milk and cookies."

Secular humanists! Henry knew he must be near a state-run college where they tell you it's okay to have abortions and draw the President looking like a monkey.

The man sobbed.

"Where are my pants?" said the woman.

Henry saw the back of a college girl in a golden sweater. There were two portions of her behind like halved peaches dipping below the sweater's hem for all the world to see. And her hair was shorter than the man's!

The man, with the sleeping bag rolled up under his arm, approached the spot where Henry was hiding, so Henry ducked and held his breath.

There was some sniffling and the like, and the woman used the Lord's name in vain and told the man to get a grip, but nobody spotted Henry and soon there came a spooky silence.

Henry raised his head and saw the sleeping bag jammed in the crook of a small tree.

All was being provided for him.

God was so good!

Henry retrieved the sleeping bag and unrolled it on the ground. He scooted in and zipped it up as far as it would go, leaving only room to breathe. He warmed up quick. The inside of the sleeping bag had a smell that Henry assumed was attempted sexual intercourse. It was pleasant, like a friendly stray dog, and foreboding, like when he had forgotten to clean out his gym locker until the end of the year. It made his pants react. Suddenly he understood everything.

Henry was like Jonah. Jesus had come to him and given him a job to do and Henry had said, No thanks, Lord, not now!

And how about Moses? "Who am I, that I should go unto Pharaoh, and that I should bring forth the children of Israel out of Egypt?"

Everybody had excuses not to follow the Lord.

"Dear God," prayed Henry, "Instead of a whale You sent an owl to scare Uncle Lipton into an episode and set me on my path. The Bible doesn't say whale, it says fish. It says a great fish, is I think how You put it. A whale is a mammal, not a fish. A whale's throat would be too small for Jonah because they just eat plankton, which is another proof that the Bible is true. So for that one occasion You made a giant fish. You could have made a whale with a big enough throat I guess but You decided not to and that is good enough for me. Everything happens for a reason. Like the hairs on our arms. Why do we have hairs on our arms? Hairs are sensory devices that help with the senses. Please forgive me for when I said in Bible study that I believed in evolution because we have hairs on our arms. So what? Charles Darwin converted on his deathbed. He was like, 'I have totally fouled things up.' He admitted it was all a big mistake. He said he was sorry for messing with people's heads. Now I am sure he is in Heaven because a person could like murder a million people and then accept the Savior into their heart on their deathbed and Jesus will be like, 'Cool.' But that is no excuse to do bad things. You can't be like, 'Ha ha, I am going to kill this person and later on I will ask God to forgive me and I will totally go to heaven.' That doesn't cut it. Nobody can trick You, Lord. You are not into loopholes. From now on I'm going to do whatever You say. You ordered me to help Polly Finch and I ignored You, Lord. I tried to tell myself I was mistaken. Like why would You look like Luke from *Gilmore Girls*? He is nothing but a big grump. Why does he get to date Lorelai? Please make him stop. What else? Please help Uncle Lipton to get better if that is in Your eternal plan. If not, well, okay, that's Your call, but it sure would be a drag. And before I forget, thank You for providing me with this sleeping bag just as You provided the Israelites with manna from heaven. You sent a pillar of fire to guide them by night. I'm just like those Israelites because I don't know where Your commandment will take me, Lord. I don't know what hardships may lay on the road between me and Polly Finch. I don't even know where Upstate New York is, come to think about it. All I can do is stay alert for any signs You see fit to bring unto me. I don't expect a pillar of fire, but if You decided to give me one that would be cool. I would totally love to see one. Please forgive me for all my sins and protect me on this journey with the presence of Your holy angels. In Jesus's holy and precious name I pray, Amen."

7

"Somebody's been sleeping in my sleeping bag."

Henry woke, nudged by a foot.

"Sorry, mister," he said. He scrambled part way out.

"Mister? How old are you, dude?"

"Fourteen."

"Dude. Me too!"

The boy had kinky black hair instead of straight, his voice was deeper, his complexion was better, and it looked as if he were trying to grow a moustache—but otherwise he might have been Henry's twin.

"So are you like homeless or whatever?"

"Yes," said Henry.

"That sucks. Well, I'm out of here. It's fine if you want to use the sleeping bag or whatever? As long as you don't steal it. I use it to bag these college chicks. They love doing it outside. They're like animals. I'm from New Jersey. They're not like that up there. Up there we got civilization. If I told you what I was doing in that sleeping bag a few minutes ago you wouldn't believe it. Sorry, dude. I'm like wired from doing it so much."

Henry settled back into the sleeping bag.

"Just roll it up and leave it where you found it. Can I trust you, dude?"

"Yes," said Henry.

"Because that's like a hundred-dollar sleeping bag."

The boy held a pack of cigarettes down toward the bag.

"No thank you," said Henry.

"Dude! You are like one polite homeless person."

The boy lit a cigarette for himself.

"Okay, I better get out of here. Hey, should I like bring you some food tomorrow morning or whatever?"

"No thank you. I'll be fine."

"Right. Well, you know, take it easy or whatever."

Henry settled down and zipped himself in, tight and warm. He heard the boy walking away and pretty soon he heard him walking back.

"This is stupid. Why don't you come stay at my aunt and uncle's place tonight? You can like sleep in the garage or whatever. There's a space heater. You can get something to eat. You won't rob them or kill them or anything will you?"

"No," said Henry.

"That's cool."

8

They were walking to the aunt and uncle's house.

"I'm staying with them while my parents are in Venezuela or somewhere monitoring human rights violations," said the boy, whose name was Vince. "My uncle teaches art history at the college. He brings his classes over to the house sometimes and that's how I bag my college chicks. These Southern dudes are too repressed to give them what they want. Like a fourteen-year-old Jersey dude is the equivalent of a twenty-six-year-old Southern dude? That's an estimate."

"My uncle's gone to London, England, with an exploding sore in his brain," said Henry.

"Ouch."

"He's not my uncle. He's my mother's uncle. My great-uncle."

"Yeah, thanks for clearing that up, dude. That's like valuable information. That'll like come in handy if I ever have to write your autobiography."

Vince flicked away his cigarette in an impressive motion such as Henry had seen in movies about New Jersey.

9

This was what it would be like if there were no moral center. Vince's aunt and uncle had naked pictures on the walls and naked statues on the tables. If something wasn't naked they didn't want anything to do with it. They ate fish for breakfast. On the morning after Vince had rescued Henry from the sleeping bag, Aunt Dora walked around in sweatpants and something like a bra. It was called a "sports bra."

Aunt Dora had been on her way out to run in the city streets halfway naked first thing in the morning when she had noticed Henry watching cartoons with Vince and offered to whip up some breakfast. That was nice of her, but she could have put on a robe or something to cover her nakedness. She was probably about forty and had to wear glasses from infirmity but just flaunted her nakedness unashamed and the lemony dots in the narrowing pale scoop of her underarm when she reached to get a mixing bowl made Henry feel feelings.

The uncle had a tall, bald forehead but long orange-and-silver hair in the back, pulled into a ponytail such as was popularized by the fore-fathers of our nation. He grew a wiry patch under his bottom lip like a drug dealer might have worn and had a silvery devil beard, and he cursed openly with a big smile on his face in front of young people like it was the most acceptable thing in the world. He put alcohol in his tomato juice in front of everybody.

Neither the aunt nor the uncle objected to the music that Vince blasted through the house during breakfast, rap music in which unhealthy sentiments were endorsed in the dirtiest language that Henry had ever heard. The authority figures even pretended to enjoy the rap music. Nobody asked Henry who he was or who his family was or why he was there or when he had shown up because apparently they had abandoned the concepts of responsibility and discipline.

Henry didn't know whether to use a fork or a spoon on any particular thing. Just two years earlier Daphne Bates had seen him pick up a pork chop and eat it with his hands and that had made the whole year of seventh grade a nightmare. Everybody had started calling him Pork Chop. Some people still did. He used to go home and pray every night that God would erase the pork chop from everybody's memory. It didn't seem like too much to ask compared to making the sun stand still, which God had done one time for Joshua, no problem. Henry finally came to understand that his prayer had been based on pride, which was why it had been answered "no." It wasn't God's fault that Henry had picked up a pork chop with his hands. That was like when these atheists on TV started whining and complaining about "How can God allow a little child to starve?" Hey, I've got an idea, give the child a sandwich and shut up, atheist. In some ways, Henry felt that he was no better than an atheist.

"Is everything all right, Henry?"

"Yes ma'am."

"Well then, go ahead and eat! Don't wait for me. French politeness!

Respect for the food!"

Everyone seemed to think that Aunt Dora had made a wonderful comment. All three of them, including Aunt Dora, laughed and laughed. Henry didn't understand. Was it a joke? The French had not supported the war on terrorism. Was it something to do with that? These people probably wished they were in France right now, making fun of the President and going number two on the American flag. He suddenly had an image of the three of them lined up squatting in a row according to height, all laughing and smiling and going number two on a large American flag spread out on the ground. It was an image that was wrong in so many ways. He could see the sandy garden of Aunt Dora's welcoming vulva, for example.

"My goodness, that fellow certainly does want to 'pop a cap' in the posterior region of that 'bee-yotch,' does he not?" said the uncle, referring to the rap performance underway.

Vince shrugged.

"You're one of Vince's 'homeys,' eh, chief?"

"Yes sir."

"Sir! I find that insulting. Call me Duffy. Everybody else does."

"I don't," said Aunt Dora.

"I don't," said Vince.

"Oh, you guys. You know what I mean. My students do. The 'kids,' or 'home slices' as I refer to them, believe me to be quite 'hep' in that fashion."

"What a loser," said Vince.

"Now Vince, what I have I told you about describing your uncle so accurately?"

Aunt Dora spooned something yellow into a bowl while everyone howled with laughter over her disrespect for the head of the household. Duffy said a bunch of stuff that apparently came out of an old movie nobody had ever heard of. Everybody rolled their eyes at him, right to his face.

"Aren't you hungry?" Aunt Dora asked Henry.

"Hurt my tongue," said Henry.

"Maybe you could have the polenta," said Aunt Dora.

"Which one's a polenta?" said Henry.

Duffy drained his coffee.

"Sorry," he said, "but I'll have to leave it to you gastronomic Magellans to explore that one. Duty calls."

He got up.

"Where are you going? You don't have class today," said Aunt Dora.

"No, not exactly. Didn't I tell you? I'm taking some of the 'leaders of tomorrow' on a 'real trippy scene.'"

Duffy had promised, it seemed, to drive some of his students to a special event an hour north of the city and he had forgotten to tell Aunt Dora, though he could have sworn he had mentioned something.

"You know, Scarecrow Farm," said Duffy.

"I have no idea what you're talking about."

"The guy with all the scarecrows?" said Duffy. "You'll just be bored and uncomfortable and angry. I know how you feel about Brother Lampey."

"I have no idea what you're talking about. But I have a little idea what you're up to."

"Please," said Duffy.

"Where is that again?" said Vince. "That place with the scarecrows?"

"Pineknot," said Duffy. He no longer sounded cheerful. "Pineknot, Alabama. You've never heard of Pineknot, Alabama. Nobody's ever heard of it. Even the people who live there have never heard of it.

Are you happy? Is everybody happy? And by the way, can we turn down this music to a *mild roar?*"

"Ja wohl," said Aunt Dora.

"That's right, I'm a Nazi."

"Well, you're certainly acting like one."

"Yes, the main thing with the Nazis was they didn't like their music too loud. That's what was wrong with the Nazis. Thank you for the closely reasoned history lesson. Lest we forget."

"Pineknot?" said Vince. "I sure wish I could take Henry there. He's been saying how he wants to get to know the culture of his people. I know it's a school day, but…"

"You're right, Vince. It's the kind of education you can't get in a school, not in Alabama, anyway," said Aunt Dora. "This is something that means a lot to you, isn't it Henry?"

Aunt Dora had fed and comforted him—"Or what man is there of you, whom if his son ask bread, will he give him a stone? Or if he ask a fish, will he give him a serpent?"—and it seemed real important to her that Duffy shouldn't leave the house alone, so Henry nodded and pretended to understand and agree with everything she said.

Finally Duffy gave in because the permissive culture told him it was okay to be bossed around by a woman and a child. Aunt Dora got Henry dressed for the trip. She dug out some of what she called Duffy's "ancient undergrad duds" to go with Henry's good blue pants—a black turtleneck and a tweed jacket with leather patches on the sleeves.

"There. That's cute. You look just like a little professor," Aunt Dora said to Henry. "An ineffectual little professor with about as much backbone as a bowl of soup."

"That's it. Pick away at my soul, bit by bit," said Duffy.

"What? I was talking to Henry, wasn't I, Henry? Now go have fun."

"That's real Harris Tweed," said Duffy. "Look at the label if you don't believe me. That's handwoven in the Outer Hebrides from Scottish-grown wool. It's a collector's item. I don't even know if they make them anymore. We should look it up on the internet. My mentor gave it to me. Look where he burned a hole in the sleeve. He's dead now."

10

Duffy pouted all the way to the Primate Center.

Henry and Vince rode in the back of the van. Nobody talked.

They pulled up at a medical-looking building of creamy brick. A woman in a white scientist coat and slim rectangular glasses was waiting alone in the portico. Henry heard monkeys hollering and carrying on.

"Hey, Dr. Pogg," said the beautiful young dark-browed scientist.

When she had climbed in and he saw the dreamy black back of her head, Henry knew for certain that she was the girl from the golf course. He studied Vince, who was likewise fixed on her soft dark misting of hair, almost a crew cut, her almost skull-white scalp beneath it.

"The others couldn't make it, I guess. For the outing," said Duffy.

"What?"

"You remember my nephew."

"Sure...uh..."

"Vince," said Vince. "Surprised to see me?"

The girl laughed in a natural way. "Do you guys mind?" she said, passing her backpack. She smelled like a powerful handsoap that would kill anything. Henry wanted to climb over the seat and get on top of her. Her forehead was bony and exciting, exposed by her short hair and emphasized by her wild eyebrows like a couple of arrows pointing up. It almost looked like they were pointing at a pair of horns under the skin ready to emerge just at the hairline, but not in an evil way.

"And this is Vince's friend Henry. Henry, this is Josie. She's a student in one of my classes. A very gifted student, I might add."

"Hello ma'am."

"Ma'am! I'm nineteen."

"I'm sorry, ma'am."

"Well aren't you a little doll."

"We're all little dolls," said Duffy.

11

Twenty more minutes to Pineknot.

Is this where you're leading me, Jesus?

Vince would pick up Josie's backpack and smell it when he thought Henry wasn't looking.

Duffy had gotten a weird lump in his throat and he never stopped talking.

"Science is terrific. You know? I mean, I love it. The Age of Enlightenment. Am I boring you? I mean, the internal combustion engine runs on gasoline, thank you very much. How far do you think we could run this baby on prayer? Not very far, I'll tell you that. To put it scientifically, a prayer equals not even one droplet of gasoline. You know? Not one droplet! I would pay a million dollars to a person who could show me a prayer that accomplished even as much as one miniscule droplet of gasoline. Science is just, I don't know, I get excited just wrapping my mind around it. You know? My awesome comprehension of it. Look at that barn. I bet some poor jerk lives over there who thinks he could lay his hands on an empty fuel tank and make a car go. Well, not in the barn. I mean he doesn't live in the barn, of course, but somewhere. He's a type. I shouldn't have mentioned the barn. I'm making a point, okay? You and I, Josie, we understand gravity and so on. The illusion of free will caused by a slight delay of brain waves. They've proven that. We just have the *feeling* we make decisions. That doesn't bother me. I don't need angels playing harps. I enjoy the intricate beauty of physics. Molecules. Entropy. Biological imperatives and so on. Why isn't that enough for people? The glory of a sunset and so on. Because they're stupid, that's why. I'm not telling you anything you don't know, working at the Primate Center among nature's remarkable apes. You know? A sunset can be explained quite rationally without taking away the wonder of it all. Why must mankind turn it into a chariot borne aloft by winged horses? Preposterous! My brain allows me to accept the fact that the Earth revolves around the sun and so on, thus producing the lovely sunset. And various meteorological conditions and so on. Is a sunset any less lovely thereby? Of course not. And so, because I side with Galileo or Copernicus or whomever, the village priest is going to ram a hot poker somewhere unpleasant? I am quite relieved to be out of the Dark Ages, thank you very much. But in a way I'm a prisoner of my own wonderful brain, this fantastic computer that no one can understand. Take art. Art is a function of the mind. You know? Expressed through the body. The senses. There's no need to drag religion into it. *Soulful.* What does that mean? It's a word. And all these are words, these various vocally intoned grunts and inflections and so on that I'm using right now. Or are they using *me*? You know? My brain is just dishing them up, one after another with an implacable logic that I am not able to comprehend. And my body is responding by using my vocal chords and tongue and so on, my *soft palate*, et cetera, my uvula I suppose—you as a science major would know better than I!—to manufacture the appropriate physical semblance of the words that my brain is now automatically producing. It's mechanical, is what I'm saying. They've proven it at Harvard. A guy wrote a book. I'm going to get you that book as a personal gift from Amazon dot-com. It just made me think of you somehow. I haven't read it. There was a great article about it somewhere. Hey, maybe I could get us both a copy and we could read it together. Duffy's Book Club! Move over, Oprah! No, I think she's done some remarkable things. We could go somewhere cool and shady and read passages aloud to one another, is what I'm saying. As part of our tutorial. Wouldn't that be pleasant? And this other guy, the one who wrote *The End of Faith*. Have we talked about that one? What's more important, he asks us, the art and poetry of an irrational kook like William Blake, or the achievement of the guy who invented a lotion to soothe foot fungus with the wonders of scientific reasoning? Foot fungus, baby! Ding ding ding! Right answer! Now give me a hard one. I'm paraphrasing, I haven't read the book. Either book, actually. I'm using 'baby' colloquially, as a lark, I hope I didn't offend you. What was I talking about?"

"I don't know," said Josie.

"This Harvard guy, Dr. Wegner, wrote a book proving that there's no free will. That means his body robotically, automatically discovered that it did not possess free will and helplessly, automatically wrote a book about it and somehow found a publisher without being *willing* to find a publisher whatsoever. And this other person, this *End of Faith* person, Sam Harris…Hey, wasn't he the guy who won *Star Search*?"

"I don't know what that is," said Josie.

"Of course not. You're a child. A gorgeous, amazing human child. *Star Search* was like *American Idol*, but marginally more nightmarish. Hey, guess who I am. 'That was *appalling.*' No? Simon Cowell, get it? See, I'm up on the 'gangsta tip' with you young 'playas.'"

Nobody said anything. Nobody knew what to say. There was nothing to say. Duffy kind of groaned at himself before starting over.

"Well, this guy, this Sam Harris, if that is his name, he considered it *rational*, evidently, to try to change tens of thousands of years of history by going on C-Span. Okay. I mean, he's completely on the mark with his observations, but what's more rational, writing a book, *any* book, or blowing your brains out? I'll give you three guesses. The publishing world's too chickenshit to even *touch* my satirical monograph on Gauguin."

"Can we turn on the radio?" said Vince. Duffy didn't hear, or pretended not to hear.

"When you make a work of *art* it doesn't matter what you believe, quote-unquote," said Duffy. "What the artist *believes*, quote-unquote, has no bearing on the physical *reality* of the object. The guy with the scarecrows, Brother Lampey? God's not talking to him. There is no God. But because he believes in God he gets to be a quote-unquote *visionary*, quote-unquote. David Hume compared a black man of learning to a parrot that could simulate human speech, did you know that? The father of rationalism! We—white people—we're *human*, he explained with his rationalism, and black people are…something *other*. And John Brown, the religious screwball—I'm talking about a complete nut—*killed and died* for his belief in black *social* equality. You know? Not just *legal* equality, quote-unquote, like almost all the other abolitionists."

"Uh-huh," said Josie.

"What's my point?" said Duffy.

"I really couldn't tell you."

"See? My brain is too aware of itself. It's listening to itself think. Shakespeare could hold two entirely opposite universes in his mind at one time. You know? It's called a dialectic, not to get technical. Have you taken philosophy yet? You really must."

Suddenly Duffy banged his fists on the steering wheel.

"Aaah!" he said. "I wish I weren't so much like Shakespeare!"

It was Henry's duty as a Christian to witness to Duffy and bring him to the Lord. But Henry's mouth was stopped as if by an angelic presence. "How shall we sing the Lord's song in a strange land?" He could imagine expounding the gospel in a way impossible for Duffy to dispute. Duffy would pull over and everyone would kneel by the roadside. There was a painting of Jesus and the rabbis in Henry's ninth-grade biology book. Jesus was a blond kid with an awesome blue hat—Henry wondered if he could get a hat like that at J. Crew—and his robe looked so real you could see the wrinkles and everything.

It looked like that painting in Henry's head, them kneeling by the van and Henry smiling down at them in a powder-blue skullcap, one hand raised as if describing a dove in flight. "Thank you Henry for bringing us to Jesus" with tears streaming down their faces and they would go off in the bushes, just Henry and Josie, and Josie would yank down her pants and he could imagine her bunched-up white scientist coat snagged in the briars and bits of gummy pine tree bark sticking to her naked behiney.

Gum was like the living blood that came out of a tree.

For some reason that thought made Henry feel tender, melancholy, and compassionate, the way Jesus must have felt, and a torrential light filled his hollows.

12

"A *visionary!*"

They were pulling into the grounds of Scarecrow Farm and Duffy was still upset about everything.

"They took away his accreditation because he was beating the faculty with a hickory stick. An actual honest-to-God hickory stick! I'm not making this up, people. I couldn't be. Yes, ladies and gentlemen, a true visionary. I suppose I never thought of beating my colleagues with a stick because I'm not a *visionary*. Although some of them need to be beaten with something. Come to think of it, a hickory stick would do nicely. Quick, get me a hickory stick. No, I'm just venting. Violence is never cool. 'The More You Know!'" Duffy sang the last part, like that educational commercial on TV.

Scarecrow Farm wasn't a farm. It looked like a high school. Henry saw some kids getting off of a school bus and marching single file into a covered breezeway. But they weren't kids. And they weren't marching. They weren't even moving. They were frozen. They were frozen kids.

The school bus had broken windows and rotten, shredded tires.

Duffy parked next to it.

Henry looked up and saw more non-kids inside with faceless burlap bags for heads.

13

In the warehouse-like gym of corrugated green tin, a scarecrow coach forced a scarecrow kid to climb a rope while a crowd of other small scarecrows sat on aluminum bleachers, watching, eyeless. Hundreds of scarecrows, mostly child-sized, populated the yards and buildings. The indoor scarecrows were better preserved. Here and there a head had fallen off or such (Duffy explained that part of Brother Lampey's vision was never to touch the scarecrows after building and placing them, but to simply allow God to manipulate them through natural— or supernatural—occurrences), but their clothes were bright and clean and most of their poses intact and extraordinarily expressive. Duffy pointed out that almost none of the scarecrows had been built with the traditional crucifix arms; they gestured fluidly, urgently, though none of them had faces to give clues to the meanings of their gestures.

Outside, the air felt transparent, blue and urgent, the way it does in the cold part of an Alabama winter. The sun was up high and so was a smudge of moon.

The cheery snap of sunshine made the outside scarecrows scarier—bleached and brittle, they had been torn by animals or birds, trampled by real children, some had fallen like soldiers, their innards spread upon the ground, limbs broken, nests for mice, as awkward as death.

14

Duffy consulted his Brother Lampey newsletter.

"Smell this," he said, and held it practically in Henry's face.

Henry smelled the single, somewhat wadded sheet, dotted with pale purple. He smelled nothing except perhaps a vague wetness and probably not even that.

Duffy removed the paper from Henry's face and took a deep snort.

"Mimeograph. That smell takes me right back to high school. I bet you've never even heard of a mimeograph machine."

"No sir," said Henry.

"That's the smell of purple to me," said Duffy. "Kind of medicinal, kind of like moldy ink."

Duffy smelled the newsletter again.

"Lately I feel like I'm back in high school all the time. You know? It's a rotten feeling."

He looked back at Vince and Josie, who were dragging their feet, staring at the ground.

"We should head over to the football field," Duffy said to Henry. "Brother Lampey is always cryptic about his events, but I get a sense of urgency here." He rattled the paper.

"Are we the only ones?" said Henry.

"Looks that way. There may be others out at the field. I don't know. People have pretty much lost interest in Brother Lampey."

Duffy looked over his shoulder.

"Hey, you guys want to join us? I'm giving some background on the artist."

"Let me guess, he likes scarecrows," said Josie.

"Okay, never mind. You kids 'do your thing' and we'll do ours, right, Henry?"

They walked toward the leaning rust-bitten towers of stadium lights and Duffy explained to Henry about Outsider Art, looking over his shoulder every few seconds at Josie and Vince, to keep an eye on what they were doing way back there.

Outsider Art was yesterday's news, Duffy explained. For one thing nobody knew how to tell the good stuff from the bad stuff. Also, it was bound up with what was called in literary circles the "intentional fallacy;" that is, nobody knew if they liked a piece of Outsider Art until they had received a document confirming that the artist was illiterate because of undiagnosed dyslexia or a pipe lodged in his brain. Real art connoisseurs, like Duffy's friends, cared only about the principles of detached formalism, which was why they couldn't go to the movies. Duffy said whenever his friends went to the movies they found the coming attractions so atrocious and unbearable on an aesthetic level that it almost gave them a heart attack. It made them cry for the state of humanity. Other people's taste in music made them feel the same way, and places where their ignorant neighbors went to shop. It was terrible to be alive.

"You have no idea what I'm talking about, do you?" Duffy said.

"No sir," said Henry.

"Well, you're listening. And I appreciate that. I suppose I just like to hear myself talk."

Henry knew that a lot of times people just pretended to like art so they could be cool. They would stand around and drink alcohol and eat wienies on toothpicks and make a big deal about some piece of junk that was supposed to be great art, but then it would turn out to be nothing but a knocked-over garbage can or a no-smoking sign or a spot on the floor where somebody had thrown up, which was a situation that Henry had observed in many comedy movies. Like the one where the supposedly great artist had trained a monkey to ride around on a tricycle with paint on the wheels, and that was how he had made his supposedly great art!

Duffy reached down and fingered the sleeve of the tweed.

"Do you want it back?" said Henry. "Because I don't mind."

"Oh, that's very kind. No, I should divest myself of all the relics of the past. You know? Harris Tweed. Ambition. Hope. Things like that."

"Okay."

"Self-respect."

"Mm."

"Passion and so forth."

Duffy laughed (it was more like a cough) and directly thereafter went kind of slack and gray all over.

"Jesus loves you," said Henry.

Duffy seemed not to hear. They reached the broken gate to the football field in silence.

Duffy took another look around. Josie and Vince were gone.

"He died on the cross so that you might live," said Henry.

"Who did?"

"Jesus."

"Oh, right. I heard about that. Where do you think they went?"

"Maybe they're looking at scarecrows," said Henry.

"Yeah, that's probably it," said Duffy.

The self-delusion of the secular humanist! A big aching hole in his heart that only Jesus can fill!

Duffy pushed through the broken gate.

15

The football field was freshly green and white, the concrete stands sparkling with silver flecks in the sun, the groaning sentinels of the busted and bowed stadium lights lending to the freshness and sparkle a reminder of mortality.

Duffy and Henry settled about halfway up the stands. Otherwise the swept and polished seats were empty of people and of scarecrows.

Duffy pointed out the archway through which the home team had once upon a time roared forth onto the field. That opening, it was said, led not only to the locker room but to untold catacombs beneath the school grounds, where Brother Lampey lived and worked and, the rumors avowed, had put his poor football team through mysterious trials of fire and water, and training rituals of Biblical ferocity, until the State of Alabama had shut him down.

"Kind of gothic, isn't it?" said Duffy.

"Yes sir," said Henry.

"Southern grotesque."

"Hmm," said Henry. He noticed that there was a single person walking across the football field, carrying something. She seemed to be a big round lady with pink splotches on her face and big fat arms, in a black T-shirt with a colorful picture of a motorcycle on it. Her flat, yellowish hair was dragging in her eyes, which were tiny like rat eyes. When she made it to the fifty-yard line she put her contraption on the ground and pulled a microphone out of it to talk to Henry and Duffy. They had to listen hard.

"Brother Lampey asked me to tell you about his dream. He saw one hundred and eighty rams coming out right over there..." (She pointed to the great porcelain tunnel marked HOME.) "Thundering, rumbling, lumbering from beneath the ground, up a ramp and out into the open, them kind of rams that's real big and muscle-y with curled horns that look like giant cinnamon rolls. There was so many rams that they stretched all the way from one end of the football field to the other, counting their harnesses. They was four abreast. And if you will do your mathematics you will see that one hundred eighty rams could easily be divided into rows of four, just like the Lord showed it to Brother Lampey in his dream. These mighty rams was pulling on a great rolling platform, and in his dream Brother Lampey seen himself, *his own self*, at the reigns, and behind him on the platform stood the Ten Commandments, cut from the living rock, almost as big as one of those houses you see being pulled down the road on a tractor trailer, *Wide Load*. If you will come back here exactly three months to the day, on February fifteenth, you will see all these things which I has told unto you. You will see it in real life. Brother Lampey has done been invited to the Outsider Art Festival in New York City again, and this time he's up and going. They won't let us put the Ten Commandments out in front of our courthouses, but Brother Lampey intends on dragging his giant Ten Commandments all the way from Pineknot, Alabama, to New York City by the one hundred eighty spotless male rams like God showed him in his dream, praise Jesus! And as he crosses the country in his chariot pulled by rams he will gather up a mighty army of believers to bring with him into New York. And then, oh brother! I can't say what happens next, but watch out."

New York! Where Polly Finch lived! Where God had commanded Henry to go, and now He was providing the way, riding on a giant statue of the Ten Commandments. Henry realized that it was God's will he had come here—he had been following the signs without knowing it. The signs of the modern day were quiet—"And after the earthquake a fire; but the Lord was not in the fire: and after the fire a still small voice"—not like zillions of locusts and whole skeletons walking around in the street and burning wheels coming down out of the sky with eyes all over them. A sleeping bag, a tweed jacket, a crumpled newsletter, these were the signs and portents of the boring modern world—but Brother Lampey was the old kind of prophet and his army of sheep was the old kind of sign, like the moon turning to blood, and Henry would be back three months to the day to take up his role in the prophecy.

"Will you bring me back here three months from today?" said Henry.

"Are you kidding? I wouldn't miss it," said Duffy.

On the way home Duffy said to Josie, "You know what I'm going to do? I'm going to travel with that nut, however far he gets. The man of culture versus the man of instinct. And perhaps they learn a little something from one another before they're done. What a long, strange trip it will have been, to coin a phrase. I don't know, I think it's a keen angle. 'Peachy keen,' as the vernacular would have it. That's the kind of thing I could sell to a mainstream magazine, not some fusty academic journal. A Jack London kind of a thing. A man's man kind of piece. *Esquire*. I'll need an assistant, Josie. You ought to think about it. I think it could be the equivalent of a course credit. I could look into that for you. 'Easy A' as the kids say! Field work. You're a bright, talented young woman. I could really use your scientific mind on an excursion like this. Well, it's something to think about."

"Somehow I don't see myself bouncing along on a hay wagon," said Josie.

"Well, you know, we could take the civilized route. Go by way of recreational vehicle. I'm sure *Esquire* would foot the bill. Hot showers, the works. Meet up with Brother Lampey at various predetermined points. Do you like hot showers, Josie? Hot, soapy lather? Call me 'bonkers' but you seem like a hot, soapy lather 'gal' to me! Now don't get in a 'rhubarb,' 'missy!' I'm just asking because I want to go ahead and stock up on..."

"I could be your assistant," said Henry.

Duffy laughed. "There! That's the spirit!" he said.

God had everything figured out.

16

Henry stuck pretty close to Duffy and his family after having been given his Revelation. He wanted to be the kind of person that Duffy would take along on his scholarly research trip to New York, where Polly Finch lay like Sleeping Beauty, waiting.

When Henry's mother and Uncle Lipton had come back from London, England, she was glad to have the extra help looking out for Henry. She let Duffy come over and pick up Henry whenever he wanted. Then she could concentrate on trying to get Uncle Lipton to poop right.

When the time came, Henry planned to volunteer to ride with Brother Lampey for extra observation while Duffy followed behind in a bus or a van, and then at some point he would reveal to Brother Lampey that Duffy was only studying him for secular pleasure and then Brother Lampey would whip the mighty rams into a frenzy of speed and they would "lose" Duffy in an exciting chase scene, so that Henry could obey the Lord by finding Polly Finch in her hospital bed and making out with her until she woke up, or whatever it was he was supposed to do, but that was probably it.

In the meantime Henry pretended to understand and enjoy Duffy's DVDs of an old TV show where comedians daringly made fun of celebrities Henry had never heard of by singing parodies of old songs that didn't sound familiar. "It's so satirical!" Duffy kept saying, or, "What a wonderful spoof of Gore Vidal! You won't see something like that on corporate network television in this day and age," and Henry would smile and even laugh. He was being deceptive but he was also being a good sport.

Duffy told Henry a lot of things about how to holistically bolster his self-esteem despite his issues of abandonment because of his mother's increasing absence and his deformed tongue. Henry pretended to "get it."

It was true that Henry's tongue had not healed properly since the night with the owl, maybe because his mother had been too busy with Uncle Lipton to pay attention to it. The tip of Henry's tongue was split, permanently it seemed, separate sections curling away from one another like horns.

Duffy would say things like, "It's part of what makes you special as a human individual on this planet," and Henry would say, "Uh-huh." And Duffy would say, "I know a lot of 'real gone cats' who are 'totally into' piercings and tribal scarrings and would 'give their right arm'—literally! Ha ha!—to have a 'way out' tongue like that! I'm sure you're the envy of many a 'punkster.'" And Henry would run to the bathroom and cry.

Almost every night Henry sat down with Duffy to watch the Fox News Channel. Duffy watched with his laptop in his lap, firing off what he called "crank emails" to the Fox News anchors. "Listen to this," he would say, and read aloud to Henry from what he was typing, such as, "You, sir, are a cad," or "Dear Turd." Then he would laugh and laugh and have a big drink of alcohol and peer at the TV, his shaky fingers hovering over the keypad. "I'm probably on a government watch list now," he would say.

Henry pretended not to resist indoctrination, but all he was really doing was watching for a Fox News Alert that Polly Finch had popped out of her coma. And he silently prayed:

"Dear Lord, Just keep her in her coma a little while longer and I will be able to do Your Will."

Meanwhile Duffy sat in all the luxury the earthly world could offer and suffered from a broken family. The riches and attainments of a college professor are not everything! Aunt Dora was never home. She had begun to enjoy trips to Mississippi for riverboat gambling. Vince never came out of his room. The situation was dysfunctional! Sometimes Josie showed up and honked her horn and Vince ran out to the car and jumped in and they drove away with Duffy watching them from the window.

On one such occasion Duffy grabbed Vince by the arm before he could get out the door.

"Ask her if she wants to come in and play Scattergories," he said.

"Yeah, right," said Vince.

After Josie's car squealed off Duffy got out his cell phone and made a call.

"Hey," he said, "I was just wondering if you wanted to come over and play Scattergories sometime. With the whole family, you know. And we could talk about those art poses I...hello? I think I lost you. Hello?"

He snapped shut his phone.

"I could have her arrested," he said to Henry.

"Sir?" said Henry.

"What do you say to a game of Scattergories, 'champ'? Looks like it's just you and me, 'podner.'"

Henry had never played Scattergories before but it didn't seem like a game for just two people and the loneliness of two people playing

Scattergories began to make him depressed. Then they were supposed to think of a color that started with "S" and Henry couldn't come up with one but Duffy said, "Sunset."

"Is sunset a color?" said Henry.

For some reason Duffy suddenly became angry and started screaming that yes sunset was a color. He said that he was an art professor and should know whether sunset was a color or not and they could just stop playing if Henry was going to challenge everything he said and he knocked the Scattergories off the table and stormed off to his room and slammed the door.

Henry picked up the pads and little pencils and everything and put them all in the box where they belonged and waited for his mother to come get him but that night she forgot.

17

Come February Uncle Lipton had to go to Texas to be hydrated by professionals. A certain amount of whispering occurred as Henry was being dropped off at Duffy's for an extended visit, and Henry couldn't help but notice that Duffy's whole family was there and acting loving. Henry felt stared at, especially after his mother drove away.

"I hope you're hungry," Duffy said to Henry. "Tonight we're going to a 'ritzy joint.' People tell me it's the 'cat's meow.'"

Aunt Dora and Vince laughed in a friendly and supportive manner and Henry felt nervous without knowing why.

18

"What's that?" said Henry, pointing at something on the menu.

"That's a baby cow raised in its own excrement," said Aunt Dora.

"Tonight Henry can order anything he wants," said Duffy.

"Well, I don't want that," said Henry.

"Get something with fennel in it," said Aunt Dora. "It's crunchy when prepared properly."

"That sounds good," said Henry.

"Listen to him, already developing a palate," said Duffy. "Isn't life amazing. I'd like to propose a toast to our amazing friend Henry. Henry's mother isn't able to keep him with her for the foreseeable future, but..."

"What?" said Henry.

"Let me finish my toast," said Duffy. "Henry's mother, for various personal and financial reasons which we cannot begin to pass judgment upon..."

"Let's move on," said Aunt Dora.

Duffy smiled and cleared his throat. He put down his glass of white wine then raised it again as if beginning afresh.

"Simply put, Henry's with us now," he said with a flourish.

"Hear, hear," said Aunt Dora.

Vince, Duffy, and Aunt Dora clinked their glasses together. Henry looked down and blew bubbles through his straw into his Coca-Cola. His stomach felt like a bottomless elevator shaft.

"I want you to understand something, Henry," said Duffy. "Your mother loves you very much. She just has to be in Texas for awhile now, possibly a long while. I've been waiting for the right moment to tell you this. She has to find a job and a place to live and she just feels...Well, I guess she feels betrayed by the White House. Remember what I've told you about the state of healthcare in this country?"

"It's the band of working people like my mother," said Henry.

"Bane, not band. Bane. They mean two completely different... Weren't you...I don't even...It doesn't matter. I'm so proud of you.

You almost got it right. You know, Dora and I have never been able to…Well, what I'm trying to say is…This situation is just absolutely great for us. It's just what this family needed. You know, Henry, a family isn't just a mommy, a daddy, and baby makes three anymore. There can even be two mommies or two daddies. And the joy on Dora's face when she introduced you to the concept of fennel…I simply don't think there's any greater joy for a woman of her age to have. Or a person of her age, I should say. And Henry, who knows how long you might have gone through your young life without knowing what fennel is? Think about that. We get an amazing opportunity to impart something real…to shape a…and anyway, you're a part of that, Henry, so good for you. I just want to take this opportunity to say…" He almost started crying. Then he caught himself and raised his glass again. "To me."

The waiter interrupted.

"We're going to need a minute," said Duffy.

19

After dinner they dropped off Vince at the mall so he could do whatever he wanted without adult supervision.

Henry lay in the back seat and watched the streetlights float by and it reminded him of his father, a man he didn't even remember. He mysteriously recalled the exciting double bump and ka-chunk of driving over railroad tracks. Even the music made him think of something he couldn't remember, the radio was playing soft, a country song about killing somebody on a cold, dark night under the town hall light.

"I have to admit I'm enjoying this in somewhat of a non-ironic way," said Duffy to Aunt Dora, apparently referring to the music.

"Did you buy me from my mother?" said Henry.

Duffy turned down the radio all the way.

"What?"

"Did you buy me from my mother?"

"What a question. Yes, money exchanged hands but does that necessarily...It's semantics!"

"No, it's okay," said Henry. "'And they said one to another, Behold, this dreamer cometh. Come now therefore, and let us slay him, and cast him into some pit, and we will say, Some evil beast hath devoured him: and we shall see what will become of his dreams...Then there passed by Midianites merchantmen; and they drew and lifted up Joseph out of the pit, and sold Joseph to the Ishmeelites for twenty pieces of silver: and they brought Joseph into Egypt.'"

Duffy and Aunt Dora gave one another a look.

"I think you will find that people will tolerate your religion better if you don't continually ram it down their throats," Duffy said. "That's one thing we're going to work on."

"I'm sorry," said Henry. He sat up. "All I meant was, Joseph got sold into bondage for a purpose and I think I got sold unto you for a purpose."

"You didn't get..."

Henry leaned forward and put his hand on Duffy's shoulder. He felt shameful and sinful for what he was about to say. It wasn't a lie, exactly, but a sin of omission, which is when you let someone believe what he wants to believe.

"I'm looking forward to our trip to New York, Dad."

Duffy swerved.

"It's like you're the Ishmeelites," said Henry. "And New York is Egypt."

"New York?" said Aunt Dora.

"I swear I have no idea where he..."

"On the fifteenth, when we're going to see Brother Lampey. And he's going to ride his one hundred and eighty mighty rams to New York City and you're going to write a famous article about it for *Esquire* and I'm going to be your eyes and ears the whole way on top of the Ten Commandments."

"Oh my! That. No, that was just a...I don't know. A notion. Well, you see, Henry, now that our family is healing again, Dora and I are going to spend a couple of weeks in Belize. It's going to be just me and Dora, you understand? For the healing. Maybe we can visit New York City one day, I'm not ruling it out, you understand. I'd like to take you to see some Jasper Johns paintings in person, wouldn't that be 'neat-o'? But it won't be any time soon, I'm afraid."

"But Brother Lampey is leaving on the fifteenth."

"Henry, I've never been a big disciplinarian, but we can't have everything precisely when we want it."

"You bought me from my mother," Henry said.

He sat back, slid down some, and cried.

20

When Vince returned home, smelling sweaty and weird, Henry was lying awake in the sleeping bag on the floor of the bedroom they were going to share.

Vince turned on the light and Henry threw his arm over his red, wrinkled eyes.

"What's your major problem?" said Vince. He started rummaging through a drawer.

"Remember when your uncle said he was going to follow the Ten Commandments all the way to New York City and I could go with him?"

"No, but I believe it. He says crazy shit all the time. Like when I first moved in he said that me and him were going to build our own musical instruments from 'found materials' and be in some kind of punk band together. Then he said he was going to go down and get a cable access show for us, and he was going to build lifelike marionettes to star in it. One time he said that before he died he was going to see every animal in the dictionary in its natural habitat, in alphabetical order, even if it meant that he had to switch continents between every single animal, and then he was going to publish a sketchbook of his adventures. He just says shit. Oh yeah, we were going to build a robot that could do underground graffiti art. He was going to buy me a helicopter. I was like, 'Helicopter *lessons?*' and he was like, 'No, a helicopter. You deserve one.' That's the last I heard of it. I think he should be diagnosed with something."

"It's not fair," said Henry.

Vince found what he was looking for: a translucent orange cigarette lighter. He lit himself a cigarette, clicked off the bedroom light and landed forcefully on his bed.

"Nothing's fair," he said. "Look. He doesn't even give a crap about me anymore. Ever since I found you in that sleeping bag…"

"We're like Jacob and Esau," said Henry.

"If you say so, bro."

"I always felt bad for Esau, even though I know he was the bad guy. He sold his birthrights for a mess of pottage."

"That sucks. What do you want me to do about it?"

"If you were going to run away from home, how would that work?" said Henry.

21

Duffy and Aunt Dora had flown off to Belize for healing, leaving Henry and Vince in the care of a damp, braided woman who smelled like a cross between the candle shop at the mall and a hamper.

Vince took care of the lying and stealing.

He told the Hippie that Henry went to a progressive school where they didn't believe in grading, and that on Valentine's Day, which was secretly an Earth Goddess rite dating back to the Druids, Henry's whole class was leaving for a special kind of camp in Vermont, where at the end of two weeks, after careful preparation, they were going to sit around in a Circle of Love and levitate a silo to protest the War in Iraq. This elaborate lie somewhat baffled Henry but it sounded like a great idea for a field trip to the Hippie, who had to be dissuaded, in fact, from tagging along.

Vince also used his father's credit card to purchase a bus ticket to Pineknot for Henry. The card had been given to him in case of emergency before his own forgotten parents had left for Venezuela or somewhere to monitor human rights violations.

This was how it came to pass that Henry found himself alone on the evening of February fourteenth, sleeping in the middle of the football field on Scarecrow Farm, with nothing but the tweed coat of Duffy's mentor for a blanket, and this is how he came to be wakened on the fateful dawn by a man who could only have been Brother Lampey.

22

Henry remembered going to the circus and smelling the elephants. That was what Brother Lampey smelled like. An elephant was the behemoth referred to in the book of Job, as Henry had learned in science class. "Behold now behemoth, which I made with thee; he eateth grass as an ox. Lo now, his strength is in his loins, and his force is in the navel of his belly. He moveth his tail like a cedar: the sinews of his stones are wrapped together. His bones are as strong pieces of brass; his bones are like bars of iron…" That was Brother Lampey.

"Rise up, rise up," he said, the words like chimes, and Henry woke with his face pressed into the stiff crinkles of a black robe. Brother Lampey's thin bones *were* bars of iron as he lifted Henry from the turf.

Brother Lampey was as tall as a basketball player, long as a bone in his long gown, with a sunken marble face and eyes like yellow lanterns way behind his beak, his hair turned black from the holy ointments anointing and plastering it against his long skull, his beard tied off in two equal braids, as spidery and pervasive as fungus on a tree, reaching all the way below his waist, almost to his knees, a beard that shone with a gray that was almost the swollen purple of a thunderhead. His lips were cracked and pink and his teeth were as sharp and yellow as the toenails on his skeletal bare feet. His pointed cheeks looked like they had been scrubbed with something harsh. He looked down at Henry. White morning mist crawled around their ankles.

"Who are you, child?" said Brother Lampey.

"My name is Henry Gill. God sent me to accompany you on your journey." Brother Lampey did not seem surprised.

"Have you ever given a vitamin E pill to a ram?" he said.

"Sir?"

"It is supposed to keep their coats glossy and healthy. Do you think you could open the mouth of a mighty ram and convince him to swallow a pill?"

Brother Lampey did not wait for an answer. He started walking.

He marched toward the big opening marked HOME, to what Duffy had called the catacombs, to the darkness that Duffy had shuddered to mention as he chuckled out fumes of alcohol, to the place where nobody knew what went on. Henry was scared but he followed.

As they entered the tunnel, hot slimy balls of air, redolent of eggs and chlorine, rolled over them.

They walked under tiles a gray shade of green, lit with watery light. Presently they came to a stairwell, and Henry followed Brother Lampey down three flights of wide, flat concrete stairs. The air got cooler as they went lower and it smelled better, too, like a deluxe car wash. They came out in a vacant white hall with a dark maroon carpet. Brother Lampey led Henry to a door. He took out something that looked like a credit card and put it in a slot. A green light came on over the silver handle and Brother Lampey opened the door.

First I was in the normal world, Henry thought, and then I went into another world inside it, and then I went into a world inside that. There's a world inside the world inside the world and I wonder if there's a world inside that, and then a world inside that, and then forever and ever. I hope not.

"Take a seat."

Brother Lampey sat at his desk and Henry took the chair across from him. It was like being in the guidance counselor's office, except for the piles of old clothing and red-gold pine straw and the stacks of burlap bags and cords of wood and bundles of twigs and what appeared to be a flaccid parachute. In some ways it was even nicer than the guidance counselor's office—Brother Lampey had a microwave oven and a TV. The sound was muted, but Brother Lampey laughed at something on the screen.

"Oh yes, it is the one where Wally believes he has a pug nose."

The TV was behind Henry, so he had to twist around to see what Brother Lampey was talking about. It was an old black-and-white show.

"Wally buys a gadget that he believes will fix his pug nose. Ward attempts to assuage Wally's feelings of inadequacy by telling him of a time when Ward, as a boy, felt compelled to tape down his large ears to keep them from sticking out. Beaver innocently inquires, 'Gee, Dad, why didn't it work?,' thus implying that Ward's ears have remained noticeably irregular."

Brother Lampey laughed some more, then suddenly stopped and stared at Henry. Without taking his gaze from Henry's face he picked up a remote control and clicked off the TV.

"Are you a practicing Christian?" he said.

"Yes sir."

"Do you believe in predestination or free will?"

"Yes sir."

"Which *one*?"

"Oh! Free will, sir."

"Do you believe that a man can get into Heaven by doing good deeds?"

"No sir. Only by the grace of God."

"Would you be willing to comb out my beard?"

"Right now?"

"No, right now it is fine. But it is bound to become filled with brambles on the trail. One of your responsibilities will be the tending of it. As you can see, it is a nigh impossible task for one man. Are you good at tying braids?"

"I guess I could learn. I've seen it done."

"No matter. Are you a virgin?"

"Yes sir."

"I believe you. Shed your worldly clothing and put on this raiment of whitest samite."

Brother Lampey got up and rummaged through a filing cabinet. He came out with a terrycloth bathrobe that said "Hilton" on it and a pair of plastic yellow flip-flops.

"Thank you, sir," Henry said.

Brother Lampey told him how to get to the locker room for a shower.

When Henry was done he came back to Brother Lampey's office

wearing the robe and sandals and holding his clothes in a bunch.

"Put those on the pile," said Brother Lampey.

"That pile?" said Henry.

Brother Lampey nodded.

"Will you make a scarecrow out of them?"

"I do not tolerate questions. By my count you have asked four questions since the beginning of our acquaintance."

"Really? Four?"

Brother Lampey smiled grimly. "You remind me of the Beaver," he said. "While your blithesome manner is pleasing, it is also, I fear, indicative of a distressing immaturity in one of your years. Jerry Mathers, the actor who portrayed the Beaver, at some point bodily outstripped the character he portrayed, yet chose not to alter his interpretation of the Beaver's behavioral tics, which were more appropriate to a child of half his age. What is charming at seven, it need not be said, becomes alarming at seventeen. If you will promise to bear that lesson in mind, I shall indulge your curiosity this once."

"Okay," said Henry.

"Very well. Some discarded garments I fashion into my critters, yes. Some I burn. Some I shred and use as stuffing. The Lord often surprises me by guiding my hand in a way I do not expect. My instinct is that I will burn your particular garments. They lack the spiritual electricity that I normally require. Did you remove your underwear as well?"

"Yes sir."

"Boxers or briefs?"

"Briefs, sir."

"Then it is well that you have removed them. Had they been boxers, I may have reconsidered. Briefs, however, choke off the life and prevent the possibility of marriage. My son, my son, your clothes have changed as the flesh of man will change when Christ returns. Bid farewell to your worldly rags and tatters."

Henry looked with some sadness upon the wadded tweed jacket of Duffy's mentor. It had meant so much to Duffy, but to Brother Lampey it was not even good enough for a scarecrow! Henry thought about Duffy's mentor, whom he imagined as a chubby, sly man with a pink face, a man who drank wine that cost thirty dollars and pinched ladies on the bottom and called everybody "dear," even men. "For there is no remembrance of the wise more than the fool for ever; seeing that which now is in the days to come shall all be forgotten. And how dieth the wise man? as the fool."

Brother Lampey reached into his bottom desk drawer, pulled out a tub of Crisco and bade Henry kneel to be anointed. It reminded him of a story that the headmaster had told to the assembly, about the liberal media laughing at one of President Bush's helpers just because he liked to anoint himself with Crisco for extra holiness. Even Henry had been tempted to laugh when the headmaster said it—almost everybody in chapel had laughed, and the laughter never died out completely for the rest of the service.

But now that he was being anointed himself, he understood from personal experience that it was not funny at all to be anointed with Crisco. He was filled with a strange tingling, even in his private area, and became afraid for a minute that he might start speaking in tongues, which his church considered tacky.

23

After Henry's consecration Brother Lampey walked him over to see the Ten Commandments that they were going to ride to New York City.

On the way, Brother Lampey asked Henry if he were filled with the Spirit.

"It sure seems like it," said Henry.

"Either you are or you aren't."

"Okay then, I am."

"That does not sound convincing. Oh well. The Lord has sent you to me. I must say I am taken aback by His choice."

Brother Lampey gazed around the grounds, as if the Lord was playing a trick on him, something like a surprise party, and some other disciples were going to hop out of the bushes with big smiles on their faces. "Oh well," he said again. "My niece was set to go, but then she told me to chop off my long, long beard for it was a vanity and surely to be my downfall. She was wrong, wrong on the facts and wrong to question me, and I banished her."

"Jesus told me in person he wants me to go to New York," said Henry.

"That does not sound very likely," said Brother Lampey.

"He implied it," said Henry.

24

THOU SHALT HAVE NO OTHER DOGS
THOU SHALT NOT MAKE GRAVY
REMEMBER THE SABBATH DAY, TOM
HONOUR THEY FAT MOTHER
THOUS SHALT COMMIT ADULTERY
THO SHALT NOT BEAR FLEAS

Henry noticed several things right away: that there were only six commandments; that what few commandments there were, were incomplete and showed signs of poor penmanship; that they were not carved from "the living rock" but seemed to be Sharpied onto a brown cardboard refrigerator box tipped over on its side; that there were not one hundred and eighty bighorn sheep to pull the display, but about six or seven shabby-looking goats who smelled very bad and had a dull, evil look in their eyes. It all added up to the biggest disappointment ever. Standing there in the gym watching one of the goats nibble between a fallen scarecrow's legs and another running up and down the aluminum bleachers, letting out little round pellets of poop as he ran, pellets that pinged and echoed on the aluminum, it began to occur to Henry that here he was standing in a bathrobe and plastic sandals with Crisco in his hair and nobody knew where to find him and maybe he had made a mistake in his interpretation of God's Will.

"What's inside that refrigerator box?" said Henry. "A refrigerator?"

"That is not a refrigerator box," said Brother Lampey. "That is the Word of the Lord."

"It stinks in here real bad," Henry said. "It's making my eyes water. These goats are so loud I can't hardly concentrate. They sound like people imitating goats. It gets on my nerves."

"You have done nothing but complain and make trouble ever since your arrival," said Brother Lampey. "I do not know in whose charge you have been, but I can guarantee by my troth that he is a father of lax ways. These critters of God happen to urinate on themselves for natural causes we cannot begin to understand. And their mournful bleating is the only form of communication with which He has seen fit to bless them. Is it your intention to question the way in which God made nature?"

"I thought they were supposed to be a vast army of mighty rams," said Henry.

"I call them my mighty rams," said Brother Lampey. "I am aware that they are not rams. Mighty rams live in California and are protected under various conservation laws. Not that I feel the need to explain my ways to you, but I could not acquire a sufficient number of mighty rams for my mission, nor, indeed, a single mighty ram. Such are the vain laws of man! So I have goats, puny goats. Goats are easy to come by. You will often find a family willing to simply give away its goat for the asking, as the goat has become a nuisance, climbing on the doghouse and disturbing the family dog and so forth. Goats are intractable. You cannot stop them from climbing on things and urinating on themselves. They are devoid of personality, except for glimmerings of irritability and obstinacy. Their chief psychological characteristic is blind stupidity, for which they provide the perfect simile and parable. All the better. Just as the Lord chose for his followers the burliest of rough-hewn fishers, and even a tax collector, we will show the world that with such humble materials as a blundering goat God can proclaim to all the eternal message of His Commandments. Just as we imperfect and wretched humans may become vessels of the Holy Spirit, so may a lowly goat be called a mighty ram in service to the Lord."

Henry had to admit it sounded pretty awesome. But the general sloppiness continued to disturb him—in fact he was scared that it might be sacrilegious—and he told Brother Lampey as much in the most respectful manner possible.

"Now you are making me think of *Leave It to Beaver* again, and not in a good way!" Brother Lampey thundered. "Have you ever seen the one where Wally dallies in a beer joint with a degraded whore who practically rapes Wally in a convertible?"

"No sir," said Henry.

"It is one of the later episodes, and most uncharacteristic of the series in its vile implications. Sometimes I would rather that *not one* episode had been made, *not one*! If only to erase the existence of this foul blight from my memory. Likewise, perhaps I had best stay here, cloistered from the scorn of sinners, rather than go to New York with such an irksome companion as yourself. Perhaps, indeed, it is Satan who has sent you here to bespoil me."

"It's not him, I promise," said Henry. "I just thought, seeing the Commandments written wrong, it's not cool to do that, according to Bible teachings." He saw Brother Lampey puff up at the notion of being lectured on Bible teachings, but Henry felt that God was giving him the words: "'And if any man shall take away from the words of the book of this prophecy, God shall take away his part out of the book of life, and out of the holy city, and from the things which are written in this book.'"

"First of all," answered Brother Lampey, "I ran out of room as you can plainly see. God cannot blame me for that. If anything, He should blame the manufacturers of this flimsy refrigerator crate. Second of all, and I do not expect you to fathom this, a bit of strategic misspelling is essential to the nature of my earthly mission. Nothing pleases a wealthy heathen intellectual more than a large piece of art covered from stem to stern with ignorant neologisms and emblematic religious scrawls. Lastly, the passage to which you ascribe your fears, Revelation 22:19— Oh, yes! You see? You are not the only one here who knows his scripture chapter and verse!—refers only to the book of Revelation itself. There is no Biblical injunction regarding the artistic representation of the Ten Commandments; that is, stating that one would lose one's soul by inscribing one or two of them imperfectly onto a refrigerator carton. In any case, by your logic, I would have had to fit the entire contents of the King James Bible onto the inadequate surface of yon box. Your strictures would make religious art impractical and indeed extinct. You strike me as being something of a Muslim in that regard."

"Oh, no sir," said Henry.

"Do not interrupt me. The Lord tells us through the Apostle John to take nothing away from 'the book of this prophecy,' by which he obviously means Revelation. The Ten Commandments do not fall under his ban."

"But God always knew that Revelation was going to be part of the Bible," said Henry. "He had the Bible planned out like forever ago. So when God says 'book,' He obviously means Bible. That's just the way He is."

Brother Lampey stood frozen in thought for a moment. The gym was filled with bleating and stench, and the light from the high windows illuminated the lightly dancing particles of filth and pollution that Henry was breathing.

"I admire your ignorance," said Brother Lampey at last.

His tone suggested that it was a nice thing to say.

25

The sun was perhaps two hours shy of setting, winking at the travelers through a stand of poplars. Brother Lampey tugged a bit on the reins and blew on the slim silver whistle he used for signaling the goats. It was called a "boatswain's whistle." Brother Lampey had asked Henry to spell boatswain, which sounded like "bosun," and Henry had messed it up real bad. Then Brother Lampey had spelled it correctly—he claimed!—to show that he knew how to spell for real. But how was Henry supposed to know it was right? And why did Brother Lampey concern himself with such weird things that made him seem like a weirdo?

Henry rode beside Brother Lampey on the elevated, backless seat and the Ten Commandments rode behind. When Brother Lampey blew the whistle, the team began to slow. There were nine goats total when they had all been gathered and counted, yoked three across in three rows, trotting along obediently, pulling the modest, flat wagon that Brother Lampey called a "buckboard." There was also a tenth goat, a mascot named Little Bit, for emergency use Brother Lampey had said, such as extra pulling, or she would make good eating if things got bad. Little Bit was too small to pull much of anything, but Henry was surprised at the bigness of the other goats. He guessed he had never thought about it before. One time in fifth grade, Lance Scoggins, whose family owned a sheep farm, had started a report by saying, "If they was both standing on their hind legs, a sheep could beat up a man." Everybody had laughed at him even though he wasn't trying to be funny and they picked on him for the rest of his life, partially because he had a funny voice that sounded like somebody was pinching his nose all the time. Now Henry could see that what Lance Scoggins had said was true of goats, and was probably true of sheep, too, and he imagined going back in time and taking up for Lance Scoggins and saying, "Who cares how somebody talks?," which, shamefully, he had not done at the time, or ever. He was so weak and human, Lord!

They were headed down a bad road. Henry looked to his right and saw a row of trailers with dirty white children gaping in almost every scraggly yard. One was wearing plastic drawers and standing in a wading pool, holding an American flag. Henry waved. The kid shot him the bird.

A three-year-old who knew about the bird! And holding a flag on a wooden stick that could easily poke out his eyes! These people were obviously poor and dangerous. The goats kept slowing down, and Henry hoped that Brother Lampey wasn't stopping altogether, though he felt guilty for fearing the poor, who were one of Jesus's favorite groups.

On the other hand, wealth was nothing to be ashamed of—it was simply the external blessing of the Lord bestowed upon a faithful soul. If you were poor it was usually your own fault because you hadn't been praying hard enough. Suddenly Henry understood the phrase "white trash," which he had heard on TV from famous intellectuals like the old guy who talks about movies and the intelligent comedian with a beard. It really did mean trash, like garbage!

"We are nearing Highway 43 to Tuscaloosa," said Brother Lampey. "I expect that even a goat would have enough common sense not to run out into oncoming traffic. Nevertheless I cannot risk losing a goat. You run up ahead, into the traffic, and attempt to halt it until the safety of the goats has been assured."

Henry did as he was told.

26

They had not gotten far up Highway 43 before a state trooper skidded up the median, raising a cloud of greenish dust. Brother Lampey blew his whistle and manipulated the reins, and the goats pulled off to the side of the road and divested the land of its greenery.

A black fellow with bright green sunglasses and an impressive hat got out of the car and crossed the road. Brother Lampey motioned to Henry to stay where he was, then he scrambled down from his high seat.

The state trooper was about as tall as Brother Lampey, and much broader. They stood toe-to-toe and almost eye-to-eye. Cars crawled past. People honked and some made inappropriate comments.

"What are you supposed to be, one of the Oak Ridge Boys?" said the state trooper.

"I do not understand your cultural reference," said Brother Lampey.

"And who are you, sonny? A model for Ambercrombie and French?"

"There is no law on your paltry books about an old man driving a buckboard down the public highways," said Brother Lampey.

"First off, Oak Ridge, that ain't a buckboard."

"When the Lord God instructed me to build it, He called it by that name and instructed me in its very dimensions."

"Was that in cubits?" The state trooper laughed and then spat on the ground through the cleft in his front teeth.

"I think the Lord knows better than you what a buckboard is," said Brother Lampey.

The state trooper took out his ticket pad. "Now what I'm doing right now is, I'm writing you up for not having any warning lights, no red flags, no danger signs of any kind. Come to think of it, you're destroying state property, too. It's somebody's job to water that ditch and make it look nice." He nodded toward the grazing goats, then tore off the ticket and handed it to Brother Lampey. "Now you keep to the side of the road until you get to the exit, all right? My motto is live and let live. You can practice all the voodoo you want. Your boy there can wear a fig leaf on the main street of town, if that's the way his mama dresses him. That's called conservative libertarianism. But I can't have you snarling up my highway, is that understood?"

The state trooper held up his hand and the traffic stopped for him. He crossed the highway and sat in his car a few minutes, just a greenish silhouette behind the window glass.

The cowardly part of Henry wanted to be found in the rolls of a federal computer, identified as a missing child and sent directly to his mother in Texas. She'd have to take care of him then! But Jesus didn't want crybabies playing on his team. "Think not that I am come to send peace on earth: I came not to send peace, but a sword. For I am come to set a man at variance against his father, and the daughter against her mother...He that loveth father or mother more than me is not worthy of me..."

The state trooper started his car and took off without even saying goodbye.

"Come down here, my son," said Brother Lampey.

Henry climbed down from the wagon. Brother Lampey grabbed his shoulder so hard it hurt. Strange feelings went through Henry's sinuses and his eyes brimmed over.

"Libertarianism! Live and let live! Do you know who says that? Do you know who that was?" said Brother Lampey.

"No sir," said Henry.

"Satan, the Beast, that Old Serpent which is the devil."

"Oh my gosh," said Henry.

"Gosh is right. He seeks already to block our path. His minions will be looking for us all up and down this highway. I believe with proper whipping I could convince these goats to break through yon barbed-wire fence. Nevertheless I cannot risk one of them being scratched and subsequently suffering the ill effects of tetanus. You will therefore tear down a sufficient portion of said fence with your bare hands."

Henry did as he was told. It hurt. They crossed into the green pastureland beyond.

27

The sun fell like a bloody shawl across the Alabama fields.

The goats, which Brother Lampey had been driving with alarming force for some time in an effort to outrun the devil, had slowed again to a meditative trot when Henry spied a little farmhouse at the edge of a forest, beneath a majestic silver cross: the biggest high-voltage power pole he had ever seen. He could hear it humming with energy from across the pasture.

When they pushed open the door of the little house they found an old farmer sitting in an easy chair with the footrest raised. He had a cat the color of snuff stains on his lap. The old farmer was skinnier even than Uncle Lipton and he had patches of rough white hair too disorganized to form a beard on his skinny orange face, which was not the healthy kind of orange.

He wore overalls and a brown-and-white checkered shirt and a certain kind of cap that had been popularized in liberal Hollywood by Ashton Kutcher, a star of liberal Hollywood. It was called a "trucker's cap." Lately Ashton Kutcher had gone on TV and told everyone that the "trucker's cap" was out of fashion and he wasn't going to wear one anymore.

Ashton Kutcher had a girlfriend who was like three times his age, a movie actress from the olden days. Henry had seen her in a commercial where she was holding a surfboard and wearing a black bikini and looking real strong, like she exercised a lot. Henry thought that if he met her she might grab the most private part of his pants and just pull and yank like a mad gorilla. He would be like, "No, no, stop, it's against Jesus," and she would just look at him right in the face real serious with her jaw clenched like she was mad and keep right on yanking no matter what he said. That would be great.

"Well, come on in," said the old farmer. His trucker's cap had a picture of a scrawny rebel soldier printed on the front. The rebel soldier looked kind of like the old farmer even though it was just a cartoon holding up a tattered old rebel flag and saying, "Fergit, hell!"—referring to the Civil War and the fact that even though people would have liked for him to forget it for some reason, the old rebel soldier had decided not to forget it and he was very angry about it. The old farmer didn't look angry at all, despite the picture on his cap. The old farmer didn't look anything.

The saddest part was that he was out here in the middle of nowhere and didn't even know he was out of fashion. It was like the time his mom had taken Henry to buy his school uniform and he had accidentally walked in on an old man in the dressing room; Henry had heard a *slurp slurp slurp* coming out of one of the cubicles; he pulled back the curtain and saw a very old man, an employee of the store, hunched low to the ground on a shoe salesman's stool, eating a bowl of soup. At that moment, Henry felt exactly like Jesus, sorry for the whole world. He felt that way again as he thought of this old farmer walking around as the subject of mockery and scorn in his unfashionable cap. Then Henry realized that *he*, Henry, was the one feeling the scorn. He asked Jesus for forgiveness and immediately he could feel the scorn going away. Jesus was like Kryptonite for scorn!

"Thank you for your invitation, brother," said Brother Lampey to the old farmer. "My name is Brother Lampey and this is my young ward, Theodore Cleaver."

"Am I hearing aright?" said the old farmer, cocking his head toward the dirty window.

"Yes, there are quite a number of mighty rams outside. By mighty ram is how we arrived. They pulled us on a buckboard. I will command them to stop bellowing if you like."

"Huh. Well, I ain't got nothing against mighty rams but I wouldn't keep 'em around here too long if I was you. More for their safety than my pleasure."

The old farmer told how his wife and children had been consumed with tumors and consigned to the dust from whence they came and how his few cows had filled up with tumors and keeled over dead and his chickens had started laying tumors instead of eggs and how the corn and tomatoes and potatoes and cabbage and snap peas he tried to grow came up black and tumescent.

"Does your cat have tumors?" said Henry.

"I wouldn't doubt it," said the old farmer. "He's got kindly a bump on his head. I was just a-feeling of it. That's how come I call him

Bumpy."

"But the Lord in His mercy spared you from tumors," suggested Brother Lampey.

"I got tumors just about everywhere a body can have a tumor," said the old farmer.

"Your eyes?" said Henry.

"Yep."

"Your knees?"

"Lordy, yes."

"Your brain?"

"I reckon so. Here's a picture of it."

The old farmer reached in between his overalls and shirt and pulled out an X-ray. Henry looked at it. It didn't look like much.

"My uncle got an exploding sore in his brain," Henry said.

"Aw, that's nothing," said the old farmer.

"They took him to London, England, for it, that's how bad it was. Now he's in Texas for it and that's even worse."

"Shoot. They couldn't take me to London, England, if they wanted to. If they was to put me on an airplane I'd break in two. I got so many tumors to where I can hear 'em rattling around when I walk."

He shook one of his legs and the cat jumped off his lap.

"Did you hear that?" he said.

"Did I hear what?" said Henry.

"The tumors rattling around."

"No sir, I don't think so."

"I can hear 'em in my head. It's on account of acoustics."

The old farmer stayed in his chair, but he offered Brother Lampey and Henry the pot of navy beans on the stove. The navy beans were cold and the stove couldn't be lit and the navy beans had been sitting so long they had turned into glue. Brother Lampey and Henry sat at a card table near the old farmer's easy chair and picked at their beans in a polite manner.

There were roaches, damp-smelling magazines, little bowls of half-eaten cat food and full ashtrays everywhere. The old farmer's entire life seemed to be stuffed into one room. There was even a chair with a white plastic tub attached underneath, apparently for going to the bathroom in.

"Would you like me to pray for you, brother?" said Brother Lampey. "I could check and see if the Lord would be willing to cure you."

"Naw sir, I reckon I near about prayed my ass off at one time. Let me ast you something. Now I know God is fairly big, but He cain't keep his eyes on everything at one time, can He?"

"Why yes, He most certainly can. God has no *size* as one would conventionally think of it. Nor is God limited to our weak and fallible human perspective."

The old farmer looked disappointed by the news.

"His eye is on the sparrow," said Brother Lampey.

"That's just what I'm talking about," said the old farmer. "All them sparers He's bound to keep an eye on. Seem like that'd take up a good chunk of His time. There's probably more of them little sparers than there is human people. Or maybe I just think that because they's smaller."

"Well, friend, I think I see the problem. You are misinterpreting the Lord's Word. When Christ observes that the Lord sees even the fall of the sparrow, He is pointing out that *our* concerns as Christians are of even greater importance."

"So I reckon what you're saying is, He *has* heard my prayer and He's telling me, 'Tough titties, Charlie. You oughtn't to've lived next to them power poles if you didn't want tumors.' I reckon He's already decided I'm a goner and there ain't a blessed thing I can do about it."

"Not necessarily. When two or more are gathered in His name..."

"I reckon if everybody got their prayer nobody wouldn't never die and there wouldn't be no room to walk."

"Lay not your treasures up on earth," said Brother Lampey.

"You see any treasures around here?" said the old farmer.

"I am only saying that decay must come to us all. Don't blame God, my brother. That was the sin of Job."

"I ain't blaming God. I ain't even blaming the power poles. College feller come around here, tried to get me to sign something to where I could sue somebody or another over the power poles. Said I could get a million dollars for what them power poles done. Naw sir, I don't believe in suing. Way I see it, me and them power poles just happened to cross paths at the wrong time. If you go suing over every little thing, you'd never stop suing. Life is just one damned awful mess after another, ain't nothing you can do about it. Ain't a lawsuit in this world can make anything better. I might've got that check for a million dollars and inflicted a paper cut on myself with it and died of the gangrene long before the tumors ever got me."

"Dear Lord," said Brother Lampey, "We beseech you today to work your healing powers on this, your humble servant. He needs Your blessing, Lord, so that he might be whole again."

"I just thought of something funny," said the old farmer. "Praying is exactly like suing, ain't it? You blame the world for your problems and you ast the Judge to fix it."

"And please bless his land, O Heavenly Father, so that it might once more spring forth with the bounty of Your goodness. More importantly, please help this old sinner get over his cynical attitude toward life."

"Is that it?" said the old farmer.

"For now," said Brother Lampey.

"I don't feel no different."

"We must not expect an instantaneous miracle. Indeed we must not expect anything. It could well be that God will not cure you at all."

"Fair enough," said the old farmer.

28

Later that evening Brother Lampey and Henry spread a blanket out on the floor at the foot of the old farmer's chair, and Henry lay down to rest.

The old farmer smoked. Brother Lampey sat at the card table drinking warm tap water.

"We are looking for a way to the north," Brother Lampey said. "We are looking for a way out of the public's scrutiny. We are doing the Lord's good work, and as His Book instructs, we seek to do it in private."

"Hell of a rig you got for somebody so shy."

"I can only do as my Lord instructs me."

The old farmer closed his eyes and recited in a voice made resonant and profound by the numerous tumors through which his words were channeled and dispersed:

Better by day to sit like a sack in your chair;

Better by night to lie like a stone in your bed.

When food comes, then open your mouth;

When sleep comes, then close your eyes.

"Well, if I have ever heard of a more direct road map to the provinces of sloth and corruption I cannot recollect it," said Brother Lampey.

"Them's the words I live by."

"And look where it has led you. Words of despair, brother. Words of godlessness."

"Found it on a thought-for-the-day calendar. Weren't godless atall. Had a whole mess of upstanding Christian people on it—everybody from Winston Churchill to Mortimer Snerd. This particular one was by an old Chinaman lived about a billion years ago. I believe his name was Poor Choppy."

"If I heeded the advice of Chinamen and took to living like you, I would not today be pulling a replica of the Ten Commandments to New York City with an army of spotless rams."

"That's right, you wouldn't."

"You have made clear the disdain in which you hold my enterprise, but I ask you again: Do you know of a lonely and desolate route whereby we may travel undisturbed?"

The old farmer said that when the power company had put up the poles they had cleared a lot of land. The silver poles now stood along the way like beacons, maybe (the old farmer speculated) as far as the Tennessee Tombigbee Waterway, where all the power of Alabama came from.

"Course it's all growed up now. You'd kindly need some help to make it through the brush."

"What manner of help?"

"Say a feller with a tractor and bush hog."

"Have you a tractor and bush hog?"

"I'm a farmer ain't I?"

"Do you dangle these items in front of me wherefore to mock my faith or do you intend to come to our aid and do the work of the Lord?"

"First time anybody's ast me to do anything in fifteen, twenty years. I reckon Poor Choppy would approve on principle. Go with the flow, that's his motto, I reckon."

The next morning, the old farmer traveled a good ways ahead of them "making the crooked places straight" like John the Baptist, taking down saplings and brambles in the path of the goat cart with the bush hog he towed behind his tractor. Occasionally the bush hog would sling up a snake that whipped through the air and landed in the path of the goats, who trampled it underfoot like the Lamb of God bruising the head of the Old Serpent. Henry hadn't been sure that the snakes were snakes at first; it was hard to tell through the binoculars.

The binoculars came from under the buckboard. Perhaps they had been strapped there with ropes. Henry didn't know because Brother Lampey made him swear not to look under the buckboard for any reason, ever. The bottom of the buckboard was hung all about with a thick purple fabric such as you might make curtains out of, and when Brother Lampey slipped under to fetch something he acquired all the secrecy of a Levite priest.

From time to time Brother Lampey would crawl under and come out with all kinds of things—the binoculars, a can of gasoline for the tractor, a checkerboard, a 12-pack of Charmin Ultra. On the first night, after they had made camp, Henry asked if he could use some of the toilet paper and Brother Lampey said there wasn't any. Henry accepted the answer though he could not figure how the whole 12-pack could be gone, nor could he understand why Brother Lampey would lie about such a thing. Brother Lampey suggested that Henry use a pinecone. It was good enough for Brother Lampey when he was a boy. The old farmer agreed that there was nothing so marvelous and apt as a pinecone for sanitary purposes. Toilet paper was only a scheme for some crooked paper mill owner to get rich by, playing on the snobbery of college-educated elitists who thought their butts were too good for a pinecone.

Henry went into a thicket, looking for a good place to go number two, and he could hear Brother Lampey and the old farmer laughing in the clearing. He felt around on the ground for a pinecone but all he could find was a pointy stick.

29

A cool spell was followed by a nice warm spell, and in any case Henry's robe was surprisingly comfortable in a chill (thanks to the terrycloth) or in the heat of the day (its breezy looseness). Sleeping outside was kind of fun and Bumpy the Cat, who rode by day on the old farmer's lap, took a liking to Henry and usually slept on his chest at night, making friendly pawing motions as though he was parsing out biscuit dough. Henry had never been around cats and he was surprised to discover that they were not as bad as he had heard on TV comedy shows, where the funniest thing you could do was accidentally kill somebody's cat—or if you were a very old person who died while having sexual intercourse.

One night it rained heavily and Brother Lampey produced (once again from the forbidden underside of the buckboard) a roll that unfurled into an elaborate system of sticks framing a kind of crazy quilt made of sailcloth and oilskin—more or less a tent (or "tabernacle" as Brother Lampey called it) to protect the Commandments. Once it was constructed, everybody—including the cat and a few of the goats— huddled under it and listened to the rain and thunder, feeling pretty safe there in the shadow of the Lord's Word.

30

One night, two of the goats—a black-and-white one that was the largest of the team and his meek brownish friend—became intent upon making love one with the other. Brother Lampey got a fire extinguisher from under the buckboard and sprayed them until they stopped.

The brownish one rolled around on its back, raising much dust, trying, it seemed, to rid his coat of the fire-extinguisher chemicals. The other—the one who had been in charge of the dirty deed—butted Brother Lampey to the ground and stamped on his ribs, ignoring the commands to submission signaled by the whistle. During the stamping, in fact, Brother Lampey swallowed his whistle. Henry tried to help but he couldn't get the fire extinguisher to work and anyway Brother Lampey kept screaming at him not to "tamper with the valuable equipment," even while he was being stamped into the ground.

After the stamping Henry tried to help Brother Lampey to his feet but he angrily shook Henry aside, rose to his knees, clasped together his hands and quaking with righteousness prayed very loudly:

"Lord, I do not understand your ways. You have commanded me to take unto my bosom one hundred and eighty male sheep and no female, wherefore to prevent such acts as are unclean in Thine eyes. And then You did everything in Your power to keep said rams from me, and that is how I became stuck with goats, according to Your Sacred Will. And still did I make them all males, in accordance with Your wishes, even though I could only scrape together nine. This world is nothing but a series of sordid compromises, Lord! I understand that. But so many tests, Lord! The cup You put before mine lips! What wouldst Thou have me do?"

The old farmer and Henry made themselves scarce while Brother Lampey awaited an answer from the Lord.

They ambled through the woods for a spell and the old farmer settled in a bed of lush green vines that were choking the exposed roots of an enormous crooked tree.

"What if that's poison ivy?" said Henry.

"What if it is?" said the old farmer. He lit a cigarette. His cat Bumpy came out of nowhere.

Henry smoothed out his robe and sat down on a mound of soft dirt that looked almost manmade, like a circle. The cat came over and sat next to Henry and started cleaning himself.

"Look at how he washes his face!" Henry said. "It's just like a regular person would do, just about. You could put a little washcloth in his hand and it would look like he was doing a trick."

The old farmer didn't look over. He just smoked his cigarette.

"Well, you missed it now," Henry said after awhile.

"I seen a cat wash his face before," said the old farmer. "Nothing against it."

"How you feeling this evening?" Henry said.

"Tumory," said the old farmer. He smoked his cigarette.

Henry listened to the tree frogs saying *weep weep weep*. Sooner or later Brother Lampey showed up, already talking.

"I do not wish to cause undue alarm but the Lord has made it known unto me that the goat who felled me is possessed with a devil. In ancient times the ignorant pagans believed in a man who was part goat and pranced about playing a flute effeminately. These gods as we now well know were naught but devils that roamed the earth for a spell. Tonight, as you have witnessed, a possessed goat attempted to procreate with me as if I was a woman goat. He trampled upon my breadbox, his great horned head leering, but the raiment of the Lord protected me and I wore His strength as a girdle about my loins."

Brother Lampey was shaking a little. He looked at Henry.

"Rise," he said.

Henry rose.

"You will lead the two homosexual goats deep into the woods, and there you will slay them. I have found that a large stick will slay just about anything that needs to be slain."

Brother Lampey led Henry away. The old farmer snapped his fingers a couple of times, softly, and Bumpy came running over to him to get scratched. Henry looked back. The old farmer, as he absently scratched his cat, seemed to be thinking about the rippling tops of the trees, green-black against the black-green sky.

As Brother Lampey led Henry back to the campsite he chattered in a strange new tone, kind of high-pitched, that Henry had not heard before: "I have seen the face of Satan as he tried to mount me! O, my child, we are blessed! The devil and all the pagan gods of Greece and Rome are most assuredly upset and on the run!"

With that they pushed into the clearing, where the two nodding goats were tied to a silver power pole with stout rope. Brother Lampey stopped abruptly. He threw his arm in front of Henry's chest, as Henry's mom did when she stepped on the brakes too fast.

"I can go no closer to them. I have given the deviant critters a goodly quantity of sleeping pills, but the devils stir inside them still. Do you sense it? The Evil One sets in wait for me. Go—and come back with their heads."

"How do I—"

"Go," said Brother Lampey.

Henry tugged them along and the sinful goats followed in doped obedience. It was already dark but it seemed to get darker as he went along. Low branches hit Henry in the face. He walked through spiderwebs. Everything was dead quiet except that one of the goats seemed to be snoring as it walked.

When Jesus had cast all those devils out of that one guy they had flown right into a bunch of pigs and the pigs had gone crazy and run off a cliff. Henry thought that would be awesome to see in a movie.

But why slay the goats when the demons were just going to hop into the next thing around? It could be a rabbit or a skunk or anything. How'd you like to have a skunk rear up at you and show its sharp teeth? Maybe it would say something in a deep voice. "Hello, Henry."

The larger goat stumbled or fell asleep and rolled down a hill. The rope went slack and Henry dropped it. He had to jump out of the way of the tumbling goat, which disappeared into some heavy brush. The sounds of crackling twigs and smashed shrubbery continued, becoming fainter and fainter. Henry left the second goat behind and ran to check on the one that had fallen. "How think ye? if a man have an hundred sheep, and one of them be gone astray, doth he not leave the ninety and nine, and goeth into the mountains, and seeketh that which is gone astray?"

Henry knew in his heart that he wanted to help the goat and not especially to slay it.

He pushed through the black leaves and was blinded by a glorious light.

There before him was the last silver power pole, bigger than all the rest, lording it over a chain-link fence full of thrumming, sputtering metallic caskets, furious arrangements of rods and burning beacons like jungle animals in a pen. Light flashed on the siren-red danger signs, silver sparks sprayed from the machinery.

The goat was already up and shaking its coat. It moved slowly past the power plant toward the town at the bottom of the hill.

31

"We've come to the end of the woods!"

Henry's side hurt from running. He was not sure why he was so excited. He had lost the goats entrusted unto him for vengeance but it didn't seem to matter.

The old farmer was pulling a blanket over Brother Lampey, who was asleep on the ground beside the Ten Commandments, with his hands over his head bent like claws and a look of horror on his sleeping face.

The next morning Brother Lampey seemed to have forgotten all about the homosexual goats, except for the yoking inconvenience caused by their absence. He didn't ask Henry for their severed heads or anything. He was more concerned—to the point of panic, nearly—that seven goats were not divisible by three, as nine had been. He spent several hours getting Henry to help him hook and rehook the goats in various combinations. Once he was satisfied with the arrangement they were out of the woods in twenty minutes and the goats were unyoked again to graze in the weeds. Before long, workers and their supervisors streamed out of the power plant to see what was going on. Brother Lampey started preaching them a sermon.

Henry heard the tractor crank.

Brother Lampey kept preaching. Henry ran to the edge of the woods and called to the old farmer.

"Hey!" he called.

And, "Hey! It was nice to meet you!"

And, "Hey! Mister! You forgot your cat!"

He was ignored. The old farmer simply went back the way he came, mowing down whatever he had missed the first time. It didn't seem to make a difference to him whether he was coming or going.

32

By the time they reached Demopolis people knew they were coming before they arrived. Sometimes Henry and Brother Lampey got to stay indoors, in pastors' houses. Henry got laughed at by a pastor's skinny teenage daughter for wearing a bathrobe. She was rebuked by her mother. Later Henry saw the daughter running across from the bathroom to her bedroom in a towel that was almost falling off. She saw Henry. She stopped for a second and looked right at him. She seemed to consider something. Then she ducked into the room, banging her knee on the doorframe. She said a bad word that Henry couldn't believe and slammed the door. That night he put his ear on the wall and thought he could hear her moving around. He was filled with feelings.

33

As the crowds began to increase in number along the roadsides, the Lord instructed Brother Lampey to give Henry a perm. Later the Lord instructed Brother Lampey to bleach Henry's hair, and later still to shave it all off and buy him a black wig and shave off his eyebrows also, and give him some big glasses to wear as well as special dentures to change the shape of his mouth in public. When they got right outside Birmingham there was a big sign on the Holiday Inn that said WELCOME TEN COMMANDMENTS.

The young man at check-in recognized them. He did not even object that Brother Lampey had brought in two of the smelly goats. Henry was carrying, as instructed, an extremely heavy red Bible, almost as large as Henry's torso, that Brother Lampey had fetched from under the wagon.

"Welcome, welcome. We've been expecting you!" said the clean young man.

"Do you think you could lay your hands on some beef jerky for these famished goats?" said Brother Lampey.

"I'll certainly see what I can do, sir. I just want you to know, first of all, that your accommodations are on the house. Mr. Jervis has made it quite clear that you are to be put up in our finest suite. We've set up a special awning for your rig, too, over in the Shoney's parking lot. We certainly hope you won't mind if some of the locals come to get a look at the wonderful Ten Commandments."

"I would like to give your manager this attractive Bible in recognition of his hospitality."

"Well, it certainly is a nice one, sir. My goodness, your little helper seems to have a hard time holding on to it! It certainly is a nice big Bible, sir."

"Is your manager available for consultation?"

"Oh, yes sir. What am I thinking? He asked me to send you in as soon as you arrived. Allow me to show you—"

"I can find it, thank you. And now, if you please, my goats require beef jerky."

"Oh! Of course, sir!"

The clerk helped Brother Lampey tie the goats to a revolving stand of travel brochures. The clerk went one way and Brother Lampey took the Bible and went another, leaving Henry alone except for the goats, who were eating the brochures.

Henry saw an arrow pointing the way to the swimming pool. He decided to take a look. As he was walking down the corridor he happened to see Brother Lampey standing in an office, talking to the man behind the desk—a man with no arms.

The man with no arms saw Henry.

"Yes, I've got stumps. Go ahead and get an eyeful!"

"I'm sorry," said Henry.

"This young lad was not gazing upon your stumps," said Brother Lampey. "He is merely looking for me, no doubt. He is my young ward, Theodore Cleaver by name, and he hates to be separated from me for too long of a period."

"Come in and shut the door," said the man with no arms. He still seemed angry.

Henry came in and shut the door. He stayed on the far side of the office.

"Hey, you want to climb under the desk and get a gander at my other stumps, Curious George?"

"No sir."

"Are you sure? I got a matching set."

"No thank you," said Henry.

"No thank you," the man with no arms repeated, as if it were the stupidest phrase in the world.

"Perhaps, Theodore," said Brother Lampey, "you can check and see if my lead goats have received their beef jerky. If so, you may take them outside to mingle with the other, less fortunate, goats."

"I'm not done with him yet!" screamed the man with no arms. "Hey, did you ever hear about the child-murdering abortion doctor who almost got assassinated with a Civil War cannon?"

"No sir. Is it a joke?"

The man with no arms hollered and yelped and angrily wiggled his stumps around. "It's history! It's American history!"

"Please check on the goats, Theodore."

"Don't you *dare* touch that doorknob. I'll kill you, you little SOB. I'm talking about a man whose name will never be known because he was anonymous. He didn't care about getting his name in the papers. And he just had to listen to his brother-in-law. 'I work at the Civil War museum. I can get you a real Civil War cannon.'"

"Yes," said Brother Lampey. "I believe you mentioned earlier that there was a lovely white Bible you wished to give me in exchange for the red Bible I have just now given you."

"Top of the filing cabinet. You'll have to get it yourself. In case you ain't noticed, I ain't got *no arms nor legs!*"

34

Somehow being at a Holiday Inn made Henry homesick. He followed Brother Lampey along the second-floor walkway, passing the big picture windows, some with curtains drawn, and he didn't see any actual people, but each window made Henry think of a family and what kind of life that family was having together at the Holiday Inn. He was holding on to Bumpy, who was trying to get loose.

Brother Lampey had a somewhat difficult time unlocking the hotel room because he was carrying the white Bible that the man with no arms had given him. It was just as large as, if not larger than, the red Bible he had traded it for. As soon as Brother Lampey managed to get the door open, Bumpy jumped out of Henry's arms and ran straight under one of the two king-sized beds.

Brother Lampey shut the curtains at once.

"This is the fanciest place I've ever been in my life," said Henry.

It was like a regular Holiday Inn room except bigger, and there was a fruit basket on the table near the window. Also, the door was opened onto the next room, and that was theirs, too, and it was just as big as the first one, with two *more* king-sized beds.

"Where are you going? Stay out of that room," said Brother Lampey. "That is my room."

"Wow," said Henry. "Sorry. I was just looking. This whole room is mine?" He pushed the "4" button on the air conditioner, the highest level, even though it was pretty cool outside. The blast ruffled his hair. He removed all the disguises Brother Lampey made him wear—his face-altering dentures and his large, thick eyeglasses and his black wig—and put them down on the telephone table.

"Is that okay?" he said.

"As long as you do not open the curtains," said Brother Lampey.

Brother Lampey shut the door and turned on the lights.

Henry sat on one of the beds and bounced a little.

"I am retiring in a moment into the adjoining room, which will be my room," said Brother Lampey. "You are not to disturb me. I am locking the door between us. If I need you, I will summon you. You are to leave your side of the adjoining door *unlocked*. You are not to leave the room for any purpose, and not to open the curtain without your eyewear, et cetera, in place."

"I'll need to let Bumpy out for bathroom time," said Henry.

"A cat, I believe, will hold its leavings till Doomsday if need be. For all a cat's many faults, it is an exceeding clean animal from my small understanding of it. On a related subject, it will not be necessary for you to tend to the animals tonight, so consider this a brief vacation from your chores if you wish. If I decide to have you comb out my beard as usual, I will let you know. You may watch television, but only programs of a high moral character such as *Leave It to Beaver*. If you watch the television too loudly I will bang on the wall and you will turn it off at once and leave it off for the rest of the night. No matter what kinds of sounds you hear emanating from my room you will not disturb me or ask any questions about my private activities whatsoever."

There was a kind of knock or bump that sounded as if it came from the second room, Brother Lampey's room. He hurried out, shutting and locking the common door behind him. Henry ran to the window and peeked, careful to hold most of the curtain in place.

Pressing one cheek to the window he could see just enough of the person at Brother Lampey's door to know that it was the man with no arms or legs. He was manipulating a gas-powered wheelchair with a stick he had in his mouth. That was cool. The wheelchair made a ton of blue smoke, just like the go-cart that Uncle Lipton had tried to build for

Henry when he was angry about being unemployed, and the go-cart had worked for about ten minutes and Uncle Lipton had taken it apart with an ax.

Brother Lampey's front door opened.

Henry closed the curtain. He could hear Brother Lampey and the man with no arms or legs on the walkway, talking, but he couldn't make out what they said.

Henry heard Brother Lampey's door shut. The wheelchair motor seemed to stop and idle at Henry's window for an anxious moment. It made a creepy sound like this: *Putt...putt...putt...putt.* Then it moved on.

Henry was shivering. He turned off the air conditioner.

Two beds in one room! "I can pick whichever bed I want to sleep on," he said aloud. "I wonder which one I'll pick."

It was Henry's first time alone in a motel room. He got a sudden urge to masturbate.

Masturbation is a perfectly natural urge that happens to everyone on the planet and it must be avoided at all costs, as he had learned from *Your Body Is Changing: A Christian Teen's Guide to Sexuality.* And anyway, Bumpy had come out from under the bed to sit on the little chest of drawers and stare at him. Henry couldn't masturbate with Bumpy looking at him like that. Bumpy had an intelligent face, something like a monkey face, that always made an effort to understand whatever Henry was saying.

Henry walked over and scratched Bumpy's chin. Bumpy lifted up his head and squinted with pleasure.

"Thanks, Bumpy," he said. "You kept me on the path of righteousness. I owe you one."

Henry considered that maybe he would have a nocturnal emission tonight in his sleep! That would be nobody's fault.

Was it a sin to wish for a nocturnal emission? That was kind of like wishing you would accidentally shoot and kill somebody even though you were obeying all the rules of gun safety. It was exactly like it! Nocturnal emission was not a sin and shooting someone by accident was not a crime, but fantasizing about either one was the dark poison of an evil soul.

"What's wrong with me, Bumpy?" said Henry.

Bumpy sprang off of the chest of drawers, across the room, and onto the table with the fruit basket. He pawed at the cellophane.

Henry realized with horror that Bumpy was sitting right on top of the white Bible, which Brother Lampey had left behind in his rush to answer the door.

"Bad Bumpy! No!" said Henry.

Bumpy scooted.

Henry picked up the Bible and wiped it off, even though Bumpy had left no trace of dirt. He gently dusted the embossed gold cross, the gold words *HOLY BIBLE.*

Henry sat down in the chair by the window and opened the Bible.

It wasn't a Bible.

It was a kind of satchel made to look like a Bible. There were stacks of hundred dollar bills inside. Lots of them.

Henry felt funny.

He forgot his instructions and pounded on the door he wasn't supposed to pound on. He clutched the cumbersome Bible. A spilt trail of money straggled behind him.

The door flew open.

"Have I not made myself abundantly—"

Brother Lampey saw the Bible and snatched it from Henry's hands.

"I think there's been a mistake," Henry said.

Brother Lampey came in and lay the open Bible on one of Henry's beds. He began gathering the money from the floor and stacking it back in place.

"There has been no mistake. No doubt our disfigured patron sympathizes with our mission to bring the Lord's Word to the New York art community. This is by way of a generous tithe or donation. Did not the Apostle Peter after much soul-searching accept the lodging and hospitality of Cornelius the centurion? Should we therefore turn up our noses at the modern equivalent? There is plenty of time to worry about money when you are older. Were I a young man such as yourself with nary a worldly care I would put all this behind me and watch some relaxing television programming." He snapped shut the money-filled Bible and handed Henry the remote control. Henry sat on the end of the bed and clicked on the TV. There was a commercial for a comedy show about vomiting puppets.

"See if you can find *Leave It to Beaver*. In particular the one where Wally gets a job selling red hots and soda at the lake. It would do you a world of good to see how a young man such as Wally responds to the challenges of money and responsibility. Note also the ludicrous behavior of Eddie Haskell, who would like nothing better than to sit in the sun and play his ridiculous bongos as some tepid form of rebellion. As the Lord said, 'I know thy works, that thou art neither cold nor hot: I would that thou wert cold or hot. So then because thou art lukewarm, and neither cold nor hot, I will spew thee out of my mouth.' No doubt these are the verses that the creators of *Leave It to Beaver* had in mind when they came up with Eddie Haskell. These words, no doubt, shall form the rubric for Eddie Haskell's grave. No one enjoys his bongo playing and yet to Eddie *they* are the fools."

Brother Lampey took the Bible into the other room and shut and locked the door behind him.

35

The sexiness of Henry's near-wet dream was interrupted by an ominous *putt...putt...putt,* and it was a good thing, too, because in the dream Ashton Kutcher was taking off his shirt and tossing his long, shiny hair around and Henry had some funny feelings about what might be happening next. He thought maybe he had to put his hands into a big bucket of warm, wet, white plaster and rub it all over Ashton Kutcher's chest to make some kind of statue out of him. But luckily an owl came at Henry through the dark, hung on some kind of motorized clothesline, and made him forget what he was doing.

When Henry woke, the *putt...putt...putt* was still going on. Henry's heart beat fast and hard—everything was quiet and it was all the way dark and he didn't know where he was.

It came to him. It was the wheelchair motor, idling outside his window again. Then there was a jiggle on the doorknob, Henry was almost certain, but how could a man with no arms or legs jiggle on a doorknob?

There were clicks and bumps he couldn't locate.

There were voices.

Henry sat up. He couldn't swallow. He wanted his mother. He wanted Bumpy.

"Bumpy?" he said.

He turned on the bedside lamp and turned it right back off, afraid that the man with no arms or legs would notice the light.

He noticed that the noise was gone. It hadn't faded, as far as he had heard. It was just there one second and gone the next, so suddenly that it made him wonder if he had ever heard it, if he had been waking up with part of the dream still playing in his head.

He turned on the lamp again, and looked for Bumpy.

Bumpy was in the bathtub. There was a trickle coming from the faucet and Bumpy was drinking it. It was a funny sight.

"Bumpy, you're full of surprises," said Henry. "Now come on, you're sleeping with me and that's all there is to it."

Bumpy was cooperative.

Henry was lying in bed with his arm around Bumpy, who was sleeping in a cute manner with his paws folded almost prayerfully over his face, when a telephone rang in another room. It rang and rang and rang and rang. Just when it had stopped, and Henry's heart had begun to slow, the phone rang right next to Henry's head. He grabbed it before it rang again.

"Hello?"

"Are you the person responsible for the goats?"

"I think you want to talk to Brother Lampey."

"He's not answering his phone."

"Really?"

"Are you the person responsible for the goats?"

"I *know* the goats…"

"Well, one of your goats is destroying our poolside furniture and making a racket. Would you like me to take care of it?"

"Yes, please," said Henry.

"Because I make jack shit doing this job," said the voice. "They don't pay me to catch wild animals. I'll be glad to shoot the fucker, though. Would you like me to take care of it?"

"No," said Henry.

The person hung up.

Henry put on his white robe and his yellow flip-flops. He rushed outside without his proper disguise—no glasses, no wig, no fake teeth—but when he turned the handle to go back in and get them, the door had locked itself! That's what hotel doors do! And Henry had not been given a key. He ran down the walkway, past the darkened rooms, rooms that seemed as secretive and troubling at night as they had felt comforting and wistful in the daylight, shut curtains behind which strangulation and molestation might be going on, adultery and fornication, any awful thing that happened in the dark behind locked doors.

When Henry got to the pool the poor goat was thrashing around pitifully on its side, caught in a reclining nylon lawn chair. It kicked at him as he tried to help it. Henry noticed a few things: that the goat had been tethered using a dog leash, and that the leash had snapped or been chewed; that the goat smelled sweetish, like pumpkin, which was unusual for a goat, so he had probably been shampooed and groomed, perhaps as a favor from the clean young desk clerk from earlier in the day; that the goat was the one Brother Lampey called "Little Bit," the smallest goat, with a red coat and a pure white face; that the goat was choking to death because its leash had gotten tangled around one of the bendy parts of the chair, the part that you snapped into position to adjust the angle of recline. Henry managed to remove the collar and jump back as far and as quickly as he could, the fluorescent green leash dangling free in his hand. Little Bit ran at him and tried to butt him, just like a goat in a cartoon.

"Little Bit, you're so tough!" Henry said, laughing, full of joy at saving the animal's life. He jumped out of the way and Little Bit took off through the gate.

Henry lost him.

He ran calling "Little Bit! Little Bit!" in the direction the goat had gone.

36

Henry was six city blocks away from the Holiday Inn and his chest hurt where the doctor said the estrogen had bunched up.

Henry stood wheezing air where a grove of parked cars shimmered in streetlight.

Henry couldn't believe there were this many people out this late at night. He heard a noise and saw Little Bit walking between the cars.

Henry walked quietly behind the goat, over to a red brick building and a pink neon arrow that pointed down some stairs. The arrow said, FREDDIE'S CELLAR.

Henry followed the goat down. He said, "What are you showing me, Lord?"

As he went down, step by step, he had a funny feeling, terrible and exciting, that he had locked himself out of more than his room. He felt the presence of the Lord bearing down on him, preparing him for another leg of his journey, a mystery. But who would take care of Bumpy? That was a problem. And anyway, maybe it was the devil giving him funny feelings, trying to get him off track. But something felt good, felt light and *right*, and it occurred to Henry that the good feeling came from being in a place where Brother Lampey couldn't find him. Henry had to admit some things to himself: Brother Lampey had awful breath and body odor. His robe smelled like pee. He was not courteous to other people's feelings. He was followed everywhere by flies, ants, beetles, and bees, attracted perhaps by the old, caked Crisco in his hair. The soles of Brother Lampey's feet were pure black, black as a smoker's lungs in a Public Service Announcement. The only cleanish part of him was his beard, and only because Henry combed it out every night, which took two and a half hours on average. Sometimes when Henry combed the beard various types of bugs would hop out of it onto Henry. And whenever Henry combed the beard Brother Lampey said, "Ah, aaaaaahhhh, aaaaaaaaahhhhhhhhh."

At the bottom of the stairwell there stood a beige metal door and a woman who looked like a man with her big arms folded crossly. The low, muffled boom of secular music shook the door.

"Hey," said Henry. Little Bit had nowhere to go and Henry hooked the collar around his neck.

"Hey," said the woman who looked like a man. "Dig the goat. You're one of the entertainers."

"Yes," said Henry.

She let him in.

The lights, smoke, and loud music hurt Henry's head. Freddie's Cellar was packed almost entirely with women, many of whom had short, greased-back hair.

On his way to the restroom he passed a stage quivering with red light. Someone was setting up microphones. Henry went into the restroom, let Little Bit nose around in the wet and crumpled brown paper towels on the floor, and washed his face and hands.

He looked at himself in the mirror. Seeing himself without his disguise in public was a revelation. It was different than looking in a mirror after a shower. He looked super fine as a completely bald person with no eyebrows, like some kind of celebrity who would go on VH1 and say, "I don't have a 'look,' okay? I don't care what I look like. I just have to be true to myself." He stuck out his deformed tongue. It didn't look any weirder than a lot of other stuff he had seen. It looked like something that would start a trend. Hadn't Duffy told him that before?

Henry could see also that the blue circles under his eyes were much smaller than when the trip had begun and had faded to more of a pale, pleasant violet. His complexion had cleared up to a great extent. Despite his travails with Brother Lampey his cheeks had not caved in but rather his face had filled out.

"Aren't you one of the entertainers?" he asked his reflection.

"Yes," he answered himself. "I am one of the professional entertainers."

He thought his voice sounded deeper. But he still didn't have any facial hair, which he chalked up to his hormone problem. Henry reached into the terrycloth and gingerly rubbed the lump on his chest, the bad spot with all the estrogen. He hadn't been able to go for a checkup for a long time. The bump seemed bigger than the last time he had measured it. It was kind of sore. He wasn't taking good care of his tongue, either. Sometimes there were shooting pains in it.

When Henry came out of the bathroom, the young goat in tow, people were crowded around the stage. They swayed back and forth as a woman sang. She was wearing an army jacket but she looked like somebody's mother. She played her guitar and sang a song about a flower that was sad because it couldn't smell itself.

Henry looked around. It was the first time he had been in a bar. He was filled with a strange happiness that he assumed was the sin of pride.

"Okay, Lord," he prayed. "Here's how it's going to work. I'm going to hang out here for awhile. I know this is probably a den of iniquity but maybe You have brought me here for a purpose. Hey, remember when You used to hang out with prostitutes and tax collectors? And everybody was like, 'Cut it out, Jesus.' And You were like, 'Get out of my face. I'm Jesus and I'll hang out with whoever I feel like.' Okay, I'll just hang out here, then, until I find out if I have a purpose or not. Thanks."

On his way to the bar a pretty girl with a red ponytail and red lipstick and a plaid skirt grabbed him by the arm and said something.

"What?" he said, because the music was loud.

She got close to his ear and breathed hot breath in it.

"I like your shoes," she said.

Henry looked down at the plastic sandals. They were the kind of thing a drug-addicted rock star might wear when he stumbled into a stranger's home unannounced.

"Thank you," he said.

She smiled at him, big. "You have a goat," she mouthed.

"I'm going to get some water or something," said Henry. "I don't have any money. Do you want to come with me?"

"No," said the girl.

"Okay."

The girl said something and Henry said something. They couldn't hear each other.

As Henry walked to the bar, some people petted Little Bit and some pretended it was not unusual to see a goat; they even pretended they *didn't* see a goat, like they were too cool to see a goat. It made Henry feel cool to have a goat that everyone had to pretend to be too cool to see. He went to the bar and sat down. All the other stools were empty.

Henry had a sinful attraction to the bartender. It seemed wrong because she was wearing a man's powder-blue tuxedo and had a short haircut such as was enforced on the boys at Henry's school and she looked like a slim, polite boy ready to have his picture taken at the prom, but at the same time she was definitely a girl with a girl's big eyes and deer-like throat.

Little Bit climbed onto the stool next to Henry and stood there with all four feet crowded together, perfectly balanced and seemingly content.

"Who's your friend?" said the bartender.

"A goat."

"That is correct. Your friend is a goat."

"I don't have any money," said Henry. "Can I get some water?"

"You two are with the show, I take it?"

"Yes ma'am."

"You're entitled to three free drinks."

"Can I have a Coke?"

"Sure."

She used a silver scoop to put some ice in a tall glass, then she squirted Coke into the glass with a long thin hose and used a pair of small tongs to take a slice of lemon from a white plastic box like a coffin. She flipped the lemon into the Coke in what seemed to be an expert manner.

Henry could understand the deadly attraction of bars where alcohol was served. Everything was done in such exciting ways by weird and graceful girls!

He watched the fizz dance in his glass.

A couple of people came up to the bar and ordered drinks. When they had been served and walked away, Henry said, "Excuse me, ma'am."

"What can I do for you, hon?"

"Is this an alcoholic beverage? I don't drink alcohol."

"It's just a Coke."

"I'm sorry. I've never seen anybody put a lemon in a Coca-Cola before. It just seemed like something you'd do for making an alcoholic beverage."

"I don't know what to tell you. It's a Coke. It tastes good that way."

Someone else needed her service.

Henry picked up his glass. A Coke with a slice of lemon! He sipped it. It *did* taste good that way! Henry was beginning to have bizarre experiences in the world of the flesh.

"That was awesome," he said when the bartender came back. "Can I get another one? Is there anything to eat? I don't have any money."

"We don't have a kitchen here," said the bartender. "I can give you some Cheetos."

"Okay. Thank you."

Henry drank two more Cokes with lemon and ate a large bowl of stale Cheetos. He put some of the Cheetos on the bar next to Little Bit and Little Bit ate them. He listened to the motherly woman sing more songs about the feelings of flowers.

When she was done the lights changed from red to a light blue like the color of the bartender's tuxedo.

A man with a dark moustache carried onstage a little table with legs that snapped out from underneath. The man's moustache was the kind generally seen in history books—bushy, upswept, and attached to his sideburns. He wore a leather hat and a leather vest with his muscles poking out and big goggle sunglasses that wrapped almost all the way around his head. He left the stage and came back with a cardboard box labeled PROPS, which he placed on the table. Then he stood by the table with his big arms folded. Some jolly music started playing—lots of sleigh bells and trombones and people whistling—and three girls ran out. They did stretches and jogged in place and threw shadow punches like athletes preparing for a game. One girl looked like a bottle of honey wrapped in a gray sweatshirt with some loose, shiny black pants and bright orange hightops. The second girl wore granny glasses and had on an old-fashioned flowerprint dress with a flowered hat to match—and a big muddy pair of men's brogans. The third girl, the shortest, was a slim pale gold girl with a cottontop of white-blonde hair. Henry thought she was as cute as a Q-tip with her light blue T-shirt the color of a Q-tip stem tucked into her jeans, tucked in so that it clung tight to her chest over two snowballs as Henry thought of them, cool little snowballs you could pack tight in your palm. Her eyes were so blue that Henry could see them all the way back at the bar. She stepped up to one of the microphones.

"Hi, everybody, my name is Daisychain. I just feel a wonderful spirit of love here in Birmingham, Alabama, tonight. These are my sisters-in-Spirit, Carlotta and Magna Mater, and this special and loving male being is Taylor. Collectively we call ourselves Gaia's Laughter. Thank you for coming out tonight. We do something a little different that you may not be aware of in Alabama. It's called improvisational comedy. Improvisational comedy is humorous because we use our skills in a non-hurtful way to bring you enjoyment through a communion of laughter. That communion means that we respect you, the audience, for participating with us in creating spiritually uplifting laughter through the process of improvisational comedy, which is sometimes called 'improv' for short. Really when I say 'audience' I don't mean to separate 'you' from 'us,' or to imply that we are in some position 'superior' to yours. We are all equals here in Gaia's Laughter. And that equality extends to all of you, my beautiful Alabama sisters who have come out tonight. Did you know that every time we laugh we create an opening through which the Goddess is reborn? So please join us in that important work tonight. And now, just to give you an example of how improvisational comedy—or 'improv'—works, we'd like someone to name a place or an activity."

"A coven!" someone shouted.

"A coven, beautiful! Thank you, heart sister. You're getting the hang of it already—respect yourself for that. Now will someone please give us a profession?"

People shouted things.

"I think I heard 'surfer,'" Daisychain said. "We will now present a humorous look at life in a surfing coven, with no disrespect to either surfing or covens."

The man, Taylor, trotted up to one of the microphones and began imitating the sounds of a drum and guitar playing the song "Wipeout."

Carlotta and Magna Mater stood near the back of the stage with their arms out, pretending to wobble on surfboards. When Taylor got to the yelling part of the song he yelled "Witch-out!" instead of "Wipeout!"

Nobody laughed.

"You guys don't get satire," said Taylor. "Hey, Mike Nesmith's mother invented Wite-out, did you know that? She's like a millionaire. Maybe I should have yelled 'Wite-out.' Now I wonder what that would sound like." He started making his drum sounds.

Nobody laughed. A few people groaned and complained.

Taylor stopped in the middle of his fake drumming.

"I wonder what's going on at the surfing coven today?" Daisy-chain said.

"Damn!" said Taylor. "Don't you people down here know anything? I'm from Motown, yo. We know who Mike Nesmith is, okay? He made a little movie called *Tapeheads*? He played in a little band called the Monkees? Yeah, that's right, we have this thing up North called school, maybe you've heard of it."

"Oh dear," said Daisychain.

"I remember the moon landing, okay? I saw it on my aunt's TV, yo. Who here remembers the moon landing? Raise your hands. You do have TVs down here, right? Or do you still communicate with a freaking chisel?"

Everybody started yelling at Taylor.

Carlotta, the honey-looking girl in the sweatshirt, came up behind him and put her hand on his shoulder. He turned and looked at her. She made gentle shooing motions. When he didn't move, she gave him a little shove. He stormed into the wings and disappeared. The crowd jeered and applauded.

Carlotta looked around slowly with a comical appearance such as an addled surfer might affect. She pushed her black bangs from her bright black eyes.

"Dude, where's my coven?" she said.

People had become bored and were chatting loudly.

"Okay, okay, we're going to change course here," said Carlotta. "Hello?" She tapped her finger on the microphone and things quieted down a little. "I was just wondering, is there a goat in the house?"

People looked around, laughing and pointing at Henry and Little Bit.

"I know I saw a goat in here earlier," said Carlotta. "Where's the boy with the goat?"

"I think she's talking about you, handsome," said the bartender.

Some of the women appeared to have a lot of fun roughly shoving Henry toward the stage. He was shuttled as if on a conveyor belt, his feet barely touching the floor as he was passed from one group of women to another.

"Great. Somebody give him a boost."

Strong womanly hands dug into Henry's behind, boosting him onto the stage. Little Bit followed, climbing eagerly and easily, as if he had always wanted to be a star.

Henry put his arm over his eyes to block out the spotlight. "Now I get it," he said. "This is a den of witches!"

Everybody laughed like he was part of the show.

"Excellent suggestion," said Magna Mater, the one in the big boots and flowery dress. "I believe I heard, 'abducted by witches.'"

While Daisychain frolicked with Little Bit, Magna Mater bound Henry's wrists together behind his back and tied him tightly to a chair. All his screaming, begging, praying, and attempts to escape were greeted with applause and laughter—he seemed to be, in fact, the most popular part of the act, and the more he cried for help the harder everybody laughed.

Magna Mater and Carlotta danced around his chair while Daisychain explained to the audience in her sensitive and worried voice that they were exploring negative stereotypes of female power and agency, and hoped by bringing them to the light of day through playful satire to eliminate them once and for all from human consciousness.

"No, we're really going to sacrifice him!" Magna Mater said.

The audience cheered.

"Magna Mater is amplifying the humor by pretending that she and I are at odds in this matter," Daisychain said.

Magna Mater sat in Henry's lap and vigorously rubbed his bald head.

The buttons down the front of her old-fashioned lilac dress strained at their buttonhooks. One breast pressed against him. She smelled wonderful, like seasoned flour for fried chicken.

Something began to happen in Henry's robe.

"I loved your Halloween special," Magna Mater said. "Charlie Brown, ladies and gentlemen!"

She jumped up. Carlotta leaned down, winked at Henry and patted him on the knee as if to indicate that everything was okay.

Henry was confused. His images of being castrated and hung upside down as the blood from his slit throat dripped into some sort of ceremonial dish had become contaminated with a strong and pleasurable sense of sexual temptation.

"Help! Help!" he screamed. He was vaguely aware that his cries had become, in part, theatrical.

37

Henry sat on the edge of the stage in the dark, empty club, the sleeves of his robe pushed up, examining the rope burns he had received during the show. There was a considerable amount of clinking as the bartender made her rounds, picking up stray bottles and glasses. Carlotta was somewhere in the back, collecting her "percentage of the door" from the owner.

But Henry didn't run. He stayed. He told himself it was because he couldn't find Little Bit and he had a responsibility to take care of him, and Carlotta had said, "I think the girls took him to the Lifemobile," and he didn't know what a Lifemobile was, so he had to wait for Carlotta to find out. Also, she had said, "I'm going to have a lot of money on me and I need you to protect me from evildoers in the parking lot, okay? So wait right here like a good boy." And she gave him a kiss on the cheek before she disappeared.

The Lifemobile turned out to be a white hearse with flowers painted all over it. There was a smattering of women gathered round and Magna Mater and Daisychain were selling homemade comedy CDs out of a white baby coffin.

As Carlotta and Henry were heading to the Lifemobile, somebody hissed. They saw Taylor peeking out from behind an SUV. They walked over.

"What's up?" said Taylor. He was smoking a cigarette. Carlotta took it from him, had a puff and handed it back.

She laughed. "Get a load of you. What are you doing, hiding out so the mean old lesbians don't get you?"

"You got that right."

"I swear, if you didn't own the Lifemobile..."

"It used to be the Deathmobile, yo."

"I vouched for you, dude. And then you go and..."

"I was *improvising*."

"You're just such a *man*, dude. You ought to be more aware of it. You're like such a Leo." She turned to Henry. "Why are all the men I know Leos?"

"I don't know," said Henry.

"You have to be aware of the audience, that's all," she said to Taylor. "You've seen us perform. We're one way at an Earth Day celebration and we go off in a whole other direction if it's a pro-hemp rally or Walpurgisnacht or whatever. Be *aware*."

"Hey, what about this. What about when we're doing a witch gag, I say, 'I wonder if it's really cold as a witch's tit in here,' and then I grab your tits. And I like, check a thermometer."

"How about not."

"You used to like it. You used to like checking my thermometer. My meat thermometer."

Carlotta laughed a little but didn't say anything. She bummed another drag of Taylor's cigarette.

"There's a TGI Friday's about two blocks over," he said. "You coming with? We'll have a couple of those cheesy cocktails you like in all the colors of the rainbow. Remember that Christmas Eve?"

Carlotta linked her arm around Henry's.

"I think I'll help our new friend find his goat," she said.

"Goat's in the hearse, taking a nasty, shitty nap on the seats I just cleaned at seven o'clock this morning. Come on."

"Well, I think I'll take a walk with our new friend anyway." She squeezed Henry's arm. "He saved our asses tonight, no thanks to you."

Taylor, who had not taken off his sunglasses even though he was outside at night, gave Henry a long, intimidating look up and down. Henry found himself standing tall. It was very prideful to be the object of sexual jealousy!

"Suit yourself," Taylor said. He walked away.

38

Henry and Carlotta walked into the brightly lit breezeway of the red brick building, sat on a concrete bench and studied the darkened storefronts across the way.

"A wig shop next to a Subway. And there's a lesbian bar downstairs. Is that normal for Alabama?"

"I guess so," said Henry. "This is my first time in Birmingham. I've been to Montgomery twice. All I remember is they have an ice-skating rink at the mall. That's weird. We don't have stuff like that in Mobile."

"Those wigheads are spooky, aren't they? It's like, 'This turkey sub is great. You know what? I'm in the mood to buy a wig.' What's up with that?"

"Why do they think people in Alabama are going to know how to ice skate?" said Henry. "There's no ice in Alabama. Not enough to skate on."

They sat a moment in reflection. Henry felt comfortable and intelligent, like he imagined he might feel on a date, though he had never been on one.

"You're interesting," Henry said. "I mean, your friends have interesting names."

"Magna Mater," said Carlotta.

"Was she named after the Magma Carter?"

"You're crazy!" Carlotta said, in what sounded like a flattering way. "Magna Mater is the Corn Mother. Haven't you ever heard of the Corn Mother? Demeter? The Grain Goddess? The Earth Mother?"

"I believe I've heard of that last one. I saw it on a can of chili in the store."

"Boy, you're so crazy!" said Carlotta. She pinched him and he enjoyed it. "I bet you're a Gemini. You act just like one. Did I nail it? I nailed it, didn't I?"

"Oh...no...that doesn't go with my beliefs. I wish I had this little comic book they gave me at school. Have you ever seen it? You should get ahold of one. It shows how the devil uses *Harry Potter* to trick everybody into doing astrology. Astrology is like the marijuana of the devil world. Like if you start smoking marijuana you go on to heroin and if you start doing astrology you go on to killing stuff and drinking its blood for the devil."

"I see," said Carlotta.

Suddenly Henry shook all over in a great panic. "Please don't go with the devil," he said. He grabbed her hands.

It was the first time he had held a girl's hands.

39

The parking lot had emptied. Daisychain was asleep, curled up on the front seat of the hearse with her jeans off and her thumb in her mouth. Little Bit slept beside her, most of him on the wide floorboard and his chin resting on the seat. Carlotta studied an atlas spread out on the back floor, looking so pretty as she concentrated and pushed the bangs out of her eyes. Taylor hadn't returned.

Henry sat cross-legged on one of the blue yoga mats as Magna Mater—who had changed into some red long johns with feet built into them—pulled on some yellow rubber gloves and rubbed a paste onto his wrists, which she had harmed and blistered while tying him up. "Don't rub your eyes or mouth on that until it dries. It's pretty deadly. Hey, don't worry, it's a great topical painkiller and I diluted it like crazy. I like to be on the safe side. It's monkshood I picked right here in Alabama, by the Cahaba river, so I think that's a positive thing, you know what I mean? Like you come from common soil. How does that feel?"

"Real good. Kind of cool and tingly. Hey, do you have something totally non-poisonous I could rub on my tongue?"

"Why would you want to rub something on your tongue, precious?" said Magna Mater, snapping off her gloves.

"It hurts. It hurts from time to time."

"Open up and let's see what we've got."

"No, that's okay," Henry said.

Magna Mater grabbed his mouth by force and opened it and looked inside.

"No way! You have like a forked tongue!"

"No I..."

"Hey everybody, Henry's got a snake tongue! That is so punk rock! Hey, Daisychain, wake up! Henry's got a snake tongue!"

Daisychain climbed over the seat to look at Henry's tongue. Though her water blue nightshirt reached nearly to her knees, Henry saw her white panties as she scrambled over the seat, and—hardly less astonishing—her pink legs and the clean golden soles of her dainty feet.

There was no doubt in Henry's mind that it was time for some orgies of sensual pleasure, which was when three women took off their shirts and rubbed themselves all over a male victim, usually while feeding him grapes and venison and other characteristic foods of the region.

Right now they were holding open Henry's mouth and sticking their fingers in it. Even though he was not in favor of an orgy he worried about driving them away with his Cheetos breath.

"I haven't brushed my teeth."

"Who cares? You have like a snake tongue!" said Magna Mater.

Henry was worried because he was slobbering in front of everybody. "I do not have a snake tongue," he tried to articulate. The inside of his mouth tasted like Cheetos and fingers. He began to gag, and the women took their fingers out of his mouth and passed around a towel.

"I do not have a snake tongue," Henry said more clearly.

"Dude, you should like never be ashamed of your snake tongue," said Carlotta.

"You're trying to blow my mind with your witch tricks," said Henry.

"I have no idea where you're getting this. What is it with you and witches?"

"We're just like normal college dropouts, dude."

"We've read some books."

"Some novels, some dictionaries of symbolism, no biggie."

"He just doesn't know how real women act in the real world, poor thing."

"Alabama is number something in education. Something bad."

"Are you telling us you didn't know you have a snake tongue?"

"It's not a snake tongue," said Henry. "It just looks like that because I didn't take care of it after an owl made me bite it in two."

"An owl is a messenger from the Other World," said Magna Mater.

"A snake is a symbol of wisdom," said Carlotta.

"I believe the owl is also a symbol of wisdom," said Daisychain. "What was that movie with a little owl in it? It was so cute." She knelt with a wine bottle clenched between her bare knees, pulling on the cork. Magna Mater was opening a bag of large red plastic cups.

This was just the way orgies of sensual pleasure usually started!

"A goat is the symbol of earthly pleasure, the gateway to wisdom, the chthonic penetration. Who wants some wine?"

"Alcoholic wine?" said Henry.

"Yes, sweetie."

"No thank you, it's against my religion."

"Are you a Christian, Henry?" said Daisychain.

"Yes."

"If Jesus was alive today…"

"He *is* alive today."

"I so respect what you're saying. Anyway, if He was alive today He would so be into Greenpeace. He would be, like, leading the protests so beauty products don't get tested on rabbits and everything? I so respect Jesus as a person."

"Jesus drank wine," said Carlotta.

"They have scientifically proved that the wine Jesus drank in olden times was what we now call grape juice," said Henry.

"According to you the Bible's always right, right?"

"Right."

"Well, the Bible doesn't say grape juice. It says wine. The way I remember it you can't turn around in the Bible without catching Jesus chug-a-lugging a big old bottle of wine."

"Ephesians 5:18 says 'Be not drunk with wine, wherein is excess; but be filled with the Spirit.'"

"Huh. It says be not *drunk*. It doesn't say don't drink. And anyway, if wine was just grape juice back then, how come they tell you not to get drunk on it?"

"I just don't want any, okay?"

The girls shared the bottle of wine and kept making Henry stick out his tongue so they could look at it. Then they got silly and showed him *their* tongues, which had become dark blue with wine. They fell asleep before there could be any orgies of sensual pleasure.

40

"I'm afraid something's happened to Taylor."

"Huh?" Henry woke up with one side of his face sticking to a vinyl yoga mat. He pulled loose and rolled over. Carlotta balanced on her haunches, looking at him. She shook him a little.

"Hey. Taylor never came back," she whispered.

"Mm," he said.

"Come on and help me look for him."

They left Magna Mater propped against the wall, mouth open and snoring loud, Daisychain asleep in a tangle with Little Bit, her new best friend, and in a way their embrace looked innocent and cute and in another way like a devilish horror.

It didn't take Henry and Carlotta long to find the TGI Friday's where Taylor had said he was going. There was one orphaned Honda Civic in the parking lot and no signs of life. They put their hands and eyes up to the dim restaurant windows, saw glasses lined upside down along the bar, half-sparkling in the half-light, chairs leg-up and vulnerable on the empty tables.

"Now what?" said Henry.

"Who knows? He enjoys being difficult."

She walked across the parking lot with her hands on her hips, looking back and forth as if Taylor might pop up from the flat asphalt. Henry followed her.

"I already have like a hangover. You want to sit down for a minute?" She nodded toward a strip of grass, bordered by a cement curb, that separated the TGI Friday's parking lot from a Blockbuster Video. "I just have to be near some grass, you know? There's nothing but dead pavement in Birmingham. Come on, sit down on the grass with me."

She sat down, breathed deep and sighed.

"You can literally feel your roots sinking into the earth. Your spiritual roots," she said. She patted the grass. Henry sat down next to her.

"There, isn't that nice?"

"I have allergies to lawn grass."

"Poor baby." She patted his hand.

Her hand was so soft and hot and smooth! Henry felt the blood running around in his head. He couldn't think or swallow for a minute. Carlotta took her hand away from his and hugged her knees to her chest.

Henry looked at his hand. He could feel her handprint glowing on it.

"Are you an African American?" Henry said.

"Yes, sweetie, I'm black."

"I thought so but I wasn't sure."

They found out that by a weird coincidence they both loved the old TV show *The Fresh Prince of Bel Air*. They talked about their favorite episodes, especially the ones where nerdy Carlton got to transform himself through the power of singing, then Carlotta showed Henry a trick where she bit into a Wint-O-Green Lifesaver and it made a blue-green spark in her mouth. It was hard to see because the parking lot was pretty bright with artificial purplish light and Carlotta went through half a pack of Lifesavers before Henry saw the spark. They were laughing and giggling the whole time at the foolishness of their project and the monumental effort going into it. As the Lifesavers were consumed a certain amount of playful physical contact took place. It was discovered at last that if Henry made a kind of tunnel out of his hands, and pressed them to Carlotta's face, and put his eyes to the dark tunnel he had made and then she bit down on her Wint-O-Green Lifesaver, he could indeed see the faint spark. To accomplish this, they had to be close—lying on their sides, in fact, face to face.

"Wow," said Henry. "I saw it! I really saw it!" Then he said, "Ow!" and rolled onto his back, clutching his chest.

Carlotta sat up.

"What's the matter?" she said.

Henry's hand was wet. He held it up.

"What's this?" he said.

"Oh my."

Carlotta ripped open Henry's robe.

"What's the matter with your nipple?"

"It stings. That's my bad chest. I got too much estrogen inside it."

Carlotta bent close to Henry's chest, looked at it and sniffed it. She dabbed at the wetness with her finger, sat up, smelled her finger, and put it in her mouth. Then she bent to examine him again.

"It's not blood," she said.

She flicked her tongue on Henry's chest and sat up suddenly, wiping her mouth. "Oh, sweetie, I think you're lactating."

"What?" said Henry. He tried to sit up. She pushed him back down.

"Has this ever happened before?" Carlotta said.

"No."

"Does it still hurt?"

"A little."

She leaned down, pulled the hair back from her face and went to work sucking milk out of Henry's nipple.

"Oh," said Henry. "Oh, oh."

"Is that better, sweetie?"

"I see sparks," he said.

She lapped and gulped, making little sounds like *mm, mm, mm,* until the milk stopped coming. Then she lay down on her back next to Henry, gasping a little.

41

The Blockbuster was a glorious cube of light.

When Henry woke he thought it was the sun.

But it was still night. Carlotta slept beside him on the sliver of grass.

Henry felt the lump on his chest. His nipple was raw. He closed his robe. The wet patch had dried, leaving a sour stain.

Henry got up very quietly and walked over to the Blockbuster. He saw the Cokes and Skittles in rainbow rows, the DVD packages like the beautiful tiles of a mosaic, and the TVs hanging from the ceiling with nothing on their screens but a brilliant blue. The Blockbuster was so empty and perfect in its readiness, like the Bride of Christ. "And the Spirit and the bride say, Come. And let him that heareth say, Come. And let him that is athirst come. And whosoever will, let him take the water of life freely."

Henry reached inside his robe and touched his tender spot. He turned from the Blockbuster and looked at Carlotta sleeping on the grass.

A clattering arose and a raccoon dropped out of one of the dumpsters behind TGI Friday's. It started off to the little wooded area behind the restaurant. Before it disappeared into the bushes it stopped, turned, took what looked to be a whole slice of birthday cake out of its mouth and held it in its tiny leathery hands. The raccoon stared right at Henry with glowing orange eyes like candlelight in a jack-o'lantern.

"What is a raccoon a symbol of, dear Lord? I'm sure it is something devilish—the devil makes a symbol out of just about every kind of animal, it seems like, according to those witches that You have seen fit to put me with. You have sent that raccoon to remind me to stay on track, probably, and not to be led astray by the sweet enticements of the devil. But I don't think You can say me and Carlotta did anything wrong. I don't think there's a verse in the Bible about a man giving milk."

One time a guest speaker had come to chapel to explain about the medical side of being crucified. His point had been to frame Christ's purpose in a way that teenagers could relate to—drowning in your own fluids, birds eating your eyeball and flies laying eggs in your skin—and Henry indeed appreciated the inconveniences that Jesus had faced. But of all the things the speaker mentioned, one had stuck especially in Henry's mind.

The speaker explained that the Bible is 100% compatible with logic and science, that, for example, when Christ sweated blood in the garden of Gethsemane it was a perfectly normal physiological reaction to a situation of extreme anxiety and stress—as a matter of fact, people sweated blood all the time and today's modern doctors didn't think twice about it.

From then on Henry had been constantly concerned that he might start sweating blood. The closest he had come so far was the pork chop incident, when he had prayed every night that God would wipe clean the minds of his classmates and they would forget that he had picked up the pork chop with his fingers, and one night he had prayed so hard and wept and moaned so profusely that he had to keep going into the bathroom and examining himself in the mirror to make sure he was not sweating blood.

Now Henry was praying so hard that he was worried about sweating blood again. Or what if milk started spurting out? But he had to keep praying, no matter what, until he had an answer. Should he stay with the witches just long enough to convert them? And then when they were converted should he propose to Carlotta?

Why couldn't Henry remember what Polly Finch looked like anymore? When he tried to see her he didn't know if he was really seeing *her* or the actress who had portrayed her in the TV movie or maybe even Amy Middleton from the eleventh grade. She seemed watery, like a dream. And why would Jesus look like Luke from *Gilmore Girls*? That had bothered Henry from day one.

Henry went back and knelt over Carlotta to pray. "Dear Lord, please help me to save this lost soul. I believe she would come to You, Lord, and accept Your Grace, if You would help me figure out the right things to say. She is a real nice girl who unfortunately has got mixed up with some witches who claim they're not witches. That's probably how they tripped her up. I promise if You allow me to continue on with her we will keep the milk-sucking down to a minimum. If you could help me by getting rid of that extra estrogen You put inside me and sealing off my nipple, well I sure would appreciate it and it would make my life a whole lot easier. I'm also afraid that I'm just telling myself what I want to hear because I'm so full of semen. I can't help but believe that You have burdened me in Your Wisdom with more than the normal amount of semen, and as you know, Lord, none has come out in a long time, according to Your wishes. Maybe it is a test of my devotion but I have to be honest, Lord, I don't know if I can handle it. Can't you please do something about all this semen? I'd like just enough to make a baby when the time comes and that's it. As You tell us in Hebrews, 'Marriage is honorable in all, and the bed undefiled.' Correct me if I am wrong, but I believe that means that me and Carlotta could do any kind of perverted activity we could think of once we're married and there wouldn't be anything You could do about it. That would be awesome. I can't see how it would make any difference whether I'm traveling with Carlotta or Brother Lampey. The only thing I'd have to do is get one of those witches to sweet-talk the desk man, so we could sneak Bumpy out of the room. Witches like cats. I could use Bumpy as a tool of conversion—think about it. You're going to get me where I need to go, if I know You. Maybe You only put me together with Brother Lampey so he would lead me here to this very parking lot. Yes, that's probably it. That was a good plan, Lord, and it worked great, like all

Your plans, so I guess it's no surprise. Nothing is a surprise to You, Lord. Sorry, I feel like I'm telling You stuff You already know."

Suddenly a sprinkler blossomed from the grass, puffing out like a cobra and making a noise like a rattlesnake. A spray of cold water hit Henry and Carlotta like the sprinkling that Catholics did out of their little sprinkle sticks, or the dribbling baptisms that Episcopalians forced on helpless little babies with no sense of redemption. Carlotta squealed and rolled over and laughed. Henry laughed, too, and let the water keep hitting him with its shocking coldness. It wasn't full immersion, it wasn't even close, but he realized there was some holiness to it after all, maybe not much, but some.

FINAL REMARKS

Thank you for the magnificent spread. The coffee was superlative. The tea was delicious. The water was cool. The punch was luxurious. The sandwiches were delightful. The stew was rich. The soup was memorable. The broth was invigorating. The chicken was wonderful. The beef was excellent. The pork was scrumptious. The goat was aromatic. The mutton was transcendent. The elk was tangy. The moose was tender. The duck was juicy. The ostrich was flavorful. The swan was terrific. The owl was stunning. The snake was unbelievable. The monkey brains were glorious. The tapioca was pleasing.

Many of you are here to get to know me better.

I am not the flashiest candidate. I am not the most eloquent candidate. I am not the most attractive candidate. I am not the most experienced candidate. I am not the smartest candidate.

I am not the candidate with the most teeth. I am not the candidate with the best skin. I am not the candidate with both kidneys.

I am not a generous sex partner.

I don't know the proper way to work a handsaw or light a barbecue grill.

I don't know what to say when someone dies.

Doctors tell me I am rotting from the inside out.

I'm no good with children.

I make people nervous.

I am timid.

I am vain.

But I will work for the iceman delivering the ice.

I will work for the milkman delivering the milk.

I will work for the playwright writing his plays.

I will work for the baseball player playing with his baseballs.

I will work for the housepainter painting the house.

I will work for the housekeeper keeping the house.

I will work for the bookkeeper keeping the books.

I will work for the beekeeper keeping the bees.

I will work for the shepherd herding the sheep.

I will work for the horseman manning the horse.

I will work for the dogcatcher catching the dogs.

I will work for the fisher fishing for fish.

I will work for the firefighter fighting the fire.

There is no limit to the work I will do. I love this country.

I love the mountains.

I love the rills.

I love the factories.

I love the choirs.

I love the community watch programs.

I love the self-help groups.

I love the suicide hotlines.

I love the chat rooms.

I love the escort services.

I love the rivers.

I love the rivulets.

I love the streams.

I love the trickles.

I love the raindrops.

I love the microbes.

I love the quarks.
We stand at a crossroads.
The choice is clear.
As for me, I believe in the future.
I believe in the flag.
I believe in the children.
I believe in lemon drops.
I believe in licorice whips.
I believe in rainbows.
I believe in ponies.
I believe in dreams.